A Pound of Flesh, An Ounce of Blood

A Black Love Detective Story Book 4

Antwan Floyd Sr.

A CRIME FICTION MEDIA RELEASE

A Pound of Flesh, An Ounce of Blood

Copyright © 2021 by Antwan Floyd Sr.

Dedicated to
My cousin Gary Griffin

Also By Antwan Floyd Sr.

BLACK LOVE DETECTIVE NOVELS

Piece Keeper

Cannibal in the City

Body Bags & Last Rites

Paperbacks:

Crew Love

Crew Love pt. 2 "The Black Mob"

Dope Fiction "Alpha Female"

Dope Fiction pt. 2 "Greed Between the Lines"

The Addiction "An Anthology"

Ebooks:

Wild 100's

Sperm Donor

The Last Transmission of a Gangster

12 Months of Murder: Introduction to Seduction

12 Months of Murder: Reasonable Doubt

12 Months of Murder: The Life and Times of Jade Leskiv Vol. 1

Table of Contents

Chapter One

"I was born by the river in a little tent, Oh and just like the river I've been running ever since...You know that song, Becky?" Silence. He spoke again. "No, I wouldn't imagine you would, I mean why would you? It was only perhaps one of the greatest songs of the twentieth century. Many historians call it the sound-track to the civil rights movement."

Still no response. He continued.

"That's the problem with the younger generation you don't know your history. Don't look at me like that, I'm not talking about George Washington or Thomas Jefferson or, or, or not even talking about Albert Einstein as influential as he was. The history I'm speaking of is about your *"other"* fellow Americans. You know the marginalized ones. Black history month."

He laughed. "What a joke. One freaking month, all they ever talk about is Fredrick Douglas, Harriet Tubman, John Brown, and Martin Luther King Jr. I say to hell with Black history month, hell it should be American History. I mean hell they were Americans were they not?"

Silence. "Answer me when I talk to you, child." He laughs again. "Oh, I'm sorry."

He removes the gag from her mouth. Strapped to the table by her arms and legs was a teenage blue-eyed, blonde-haired girl. He stood over her as she stared back tears streaming from her eyes and falling into her ears and nose. He sighed. "Go ahead, answer my question."

"Wha, wha...which question sir?"

He brushed her hair from her eyes with his hand, she flinched at his touch. "Don't trifle with me, child."

"I'm not sir, which question do you want me to answer the question about the song or if Fredrick Douglas, Harriet Tubman, John Brown, or Martin Luther King Jr. were American?"

He slammed his hand down on the table, the sound echoed in the empty warehouse. She flinched again and began bawling uncontrollably.

"Don't you sass me, little girl." He placed the gag back on her mouth. Stepped away from the table. Looked down at his hands, clenched them into a fist, then opened them up again. He had strong hands, he clasped them together interlocking his fingers on both hands then released and shook them off. He was a tall man, with ebony skin with a strong frame, he wore his hair cut low he had gray highlights around the edges of his black hair. He was ruggedly handsome, which he wore almost unknowingly. He walked back over to the table. Looked down at the girl. "I'm not a bad man, it's just that sometimes the world forces good men to do bad things."

He picked up a surgical blade, placed his free hand on top of her forehead to hold her in place, and ran the blade across her neck. He stared down into her eyes as he watched the pleading in them to live fade away.

***

Chapter Two

Black navigated the Black Jaguar XJ got off on Stony Island headed towards 103rd was on his way to the 4th district to meet Detective Edwards a missing person's detective. Black helped him in a previous case to find his daughter and get her back home safely, that's how he stumbled upon the string of girls coming up missing on the south side presumably victims of the cannibal. He was hoping Edwards had some information about the missing girls from the south side and if they were connected to the girls missing from New Trier. It wasn't officially Edwards's case and Black knew he should have gotten with detectives Stewart and Jones first but the way he saw it he wasn't paid by the department he could speak to whomever he pleased in whatever order he pleased. The sound of a phone ringing blared through his sound system; his phone was Bluetooth connected to his radio after two rings it was answered Parker spoke. "What's up man where are you at?" Parker was one of Black's oldest friends and new partner in the detective business.

"Headed to speak with Bunchy." That was Detective Edwards's nickname.

"Yeah, why didn't you invite me?"

"I thought you didn't like going around police?"

"I don't but if it's about getting our business off the ground, fuck em."

Black sighed. "There's nothing there, I'm just doing my due diligence, but Parker there's no case."

"If it is something there, I should be there, we both know for you being an attorney you can't negotiate a price for shit."

Black laughed. "Man, you are tripping, you know damn well that's a lie."

"Hmph, by my count you've worked on four cases and how many have you been paid for?"

"That's not fair, three of the four were family issues."

"Family gotta pay too sometimes, this is business."

"I hear you; I hear you next time I'll call you."

"Um, hmm, well I'm here alre-"

"I'll check in with you in a few hours, I have a call on the other end." Before Parker could respond Black ended the call. "Hello Ms. Malone, what can I do for you?"

Veronica Malone was an old colleague from when he worked as a district attorney. "Wanted to know how long before you made it to the station, wanted to sit in on the talks about the New Trier girls."

"I'm headed in now." He says as he pulls into an empty parking space.

"Good, I'll see you inside, I'm just getting here as well have to find a parking spot."

"See you in a few." Black ended the call, got out of the car, and made his way into the building. He nodded at the desk sergeant and continued towards the elevator, he pressed the up button and the doors opened. He stepped on and pressed the number six button and the doors closed, a few moments later the doors were opened, and he was stepping off and into the missing person department. No one paid him any particular attention he looked around the room for Bunchy, but not seeing him he stopped a detective walking by. "Hey, I'm looking for Detective Edwards."

"And you are?"

"Love, Black Love he's expecting-"

Before Black could finish his sentence as if on cue most of the officers in the room stopped what they were doing and had their guns drawn on Black!

***

Chapter Three

Parker is sitting waiting in front of the police station watching as a car pulls out of a parking space, as he shifts into reverse to parallel park into the empty spot a car zips in and steals the spot. He slams on his brakes and shifts into the park position. He jumps out of his car and slams the door closed.

"What in the hell is wrong with you?" He yells as the short thick attractive woman climbs from her car and closes the door.

"Nothing what's wrong with you?"

"Come on sweetheart you saw that was my parking spot."

She laughed. "Was it now? So, you're telling me you have an assigned parking space here?"

"Nah, but I was here first you saw that."

"Gotta be quicker than that playboy."

Parker laughs. "It's like that then?"

"It is."

"You owe me now."

She laughed. Raised an eyebrow. "Owe you how and for what?"

"Robbing me of my spot, inconveniencing my day, you owe me some time."

She folded her arms across her chest. "You're mighty confident of yourself."

Parker reached into his pocket and handed her his phone. "Put your number in there so I can call you and we can set something up."

She eyed him from head to toe for several seconds before returning his phone. "Nah."

"Nah?"

She smiled. "You never been told no before?"

"Yeah but-"

"What are you doing down here anyway, you a cop or something?"

Parker laughed. "Man, hell nah, I'm here waiting on a friend."

"Your friend on the good side or the bad side of the law?"

Parker laughed. "Depends on who you ask."

Back-to-back alerts came strumming through Veronica's phone, she removed it from her jacket pocket, clicked it open scrolled through a few messages, and stuffed it back into her jacket pocket. "I have to go, but here's my number you call me." She pulled a business card from her pocket and handed it to him. He read the card.

"Veronica Malone, District Attorney, cool. I'm Parker."

"Nice to meet you, Parker, I'll be waiting for your call." She turned and sprinted towards the entrance of the police station. Parker watched as her solid backside bounced away. He turned and headed back to his vehicle which was double-parked in traffic. Sitting behind his vehicle was an Expedition truck, the driver staring at him.

"What the fuck you looking at white boy?"

"I'll see you around home-boy." The driver says as he lets off the brakes and speeds away.

***

Chapter Four

Black sat at the interrogation table, detective Stewart sat across from him even sitting she appeared tall, dressed more like a corporate lawyer than a cop on a detective's salary, the long-haired brunette detective with a golden-brown tan didn't give off an air of aggression or arrogance. Her partner Jones paced the room, he was the complete opposite maybe it was a bad impression of a good cop/bad cop shtick. Jones was six foot two, with baby blue eyes, military-style cut blonde hair, medium-sized build his suit was tan and wrinkled, looked slept in. Detective Edwards stood in a corner with his back to the wall watching. Black locked eyes with Edwards. "Draw down on me? Really?"

"It wasn't my idea; you know the captain still has a hard-on for you about the medical files you came across while working on my daughter's case."

"What? If it wasn't for me, you guys wouldn't even have got the connection between the girls and Charles. This is bullshit!"

"You are a-"

"Suspect?"

Jones interrupted. "No, a person of interest and Detective Edwards may I remind you, you are simply here to observe."

Edwards shot daggers at Jones with his eyes, yet he ceased his dialogue with Black. A manilla folder sat in front of Stewart, she opened it and removed photos of dismembered body parts. She placed the photos in front of Black. "What can you tell us about these photos?"

"Nothing."

She removed another, it was the same as the one that Parker had shown him from the internet on his phone, a young girl's chest and stomach the arms, head, and legs were missing a message addressed to him carved in her stomach. "What about this one?"

"Same as the others, nothing."

"Nothing?"

Black didn't respond. She continued. "We have enough here to charge you."

"Then do it."

"You know with your name here carved into that girl's tummy it looks like a signature."

Black smirked. "Or a message, you'll have to do better than that detective you aren't questioning some low-level gang banger off 75th street."

Stewart leaned back in her seat. "Let's take this back a few notches, we're all on the same side, here right? I mean you were the district attorney, right? I mean you want to catch this guy just as bad as we do, right?"

"Just a second ago detective you were convinced that I was the guy that needed catching."

"I admit we were a bit overzealous with how we started this but I'm asking you if can we start this over?"

The door swung open, and Veronica entered. She was looking good 5'7, 150 lbs. of enticingly firm flesh, mocha-colored skin tone, and eyes the color of chestnuts, she wore white Pumas, and a white Puma track suit and hair pulled back into a ponytail she looked more like a tennis coach than an officer of the court. She introduced herself to the officers in the room. "I'm D.A. Malone."

Jones stepped up and offered his hand for a handshake. "Detective Jones, my partner Stewart we're both with homicide, Detective Edwards back there is with missing persons this is now a joint investigation."

Veronica nodded at everyone in the room.

"You couldn't have warned me, Veronica?" Black said after the introductions.

"I had no idea, I'll have a word with the captain later, what can you do to help us Black?"

Black laughed. "Everyone keeps asking me that help you how? I don't know any more than any of you do, I wasn't even here you know I haven't been back in this country for 24 hours and I'm being accosted."

"We're going to need all hands-on deck on this one and no one is more familiar with this Charles guy than you are as a favor to me will you help?"

Black stood from the table. "You guys got off on the wrong foot this shit is just hostile is it going to be like this during the entire investigation?"

"Of course, not," Veronica responded.

"Hmph, you noticed how you were the only one to respond and you won't even be working the case. Why shouldn't I expect more of the same? Nah, won't rope me into a frameup, give me some time to think about it."

Black made his way towards the door; Jones placed his hand on Black's chest blocking his path.

"You know district attorney Malone you need to do something about your officers this is the second time in 24 hours that detective Jones has unwarrantedly placed his hands on me."

Veronica cut her eyes at the detective, he removed his hand and stepped to the side Black walked out of the room with Veronica following close behind. As Black reached the elevator the doors opened, and a uniformed officer stepped off.

"D.A. Malone, congratulations on your run for Attorney General." The officer said as Black stepped onto the elevator, he locked eyes with Veronica shaking the officer's hand just as the doors closed.

***

Chapter Five

"Are you sure you don't want me to walk you out to your car?" The well-dressed stranger asked Ashanti as she was leaving the spoken word open mic spots on S. Clark in the Loop. It wasn't too dark, so she laughed at the thought of an escort to walk just a few feet to her car. She shook her head no. "No thank you, I can manage."

The stranger responded with a bow of the head and was on his way. Ashanti made her way through the crowd that was congregating near the exit. It had been almost two years since it happened. Her parents rarely let her go anyplace alone, one of her cousins or uncles went everywhere with her. She needed a break, a sense of normalcy after buying her a car and a handgun they finally allowed her to go out alone. She legally wasn't old enough to own the gun but that didn't matter, in Chicago, everyone had a gun she took it everywhere with her, most often leaving it in the car. She had to promise to answer all texts and phone calls no matter what. She stepped outside, she had to admit it felt good being out on her own she spotted her car across the street a two-door used Kia, wasn't much to look at but it was hers. She looked both ways before crossing then ran across the street to her car, she pressed the unlock button on the keychain, and when the locks disengaged, she grabbed the door handle and was about to get in when a black SUV pulled next to her and stopped, she looked at the driver only to find a gun pointed in her face.

"Flash a smile, close your car door, and get in with me or I'm going to leave your brains on the side of your driver's door."

Ashanti froze.

"I don't have all day."

"It's you!"

"You have until the count of two, sweetheart."

"One-"

Ashanti did as she was told, closed her car door, opened the truck door, climbed in, and closed the door the truck pulled off just as others from the club began exiting.

***

Chapter Six

After the not-so-smooth interaction with Black and the room full of detectives earlier that day, Veronica rushed over to play a few games of squash with friends of hers, after a few drinks in the lounge of the Racquet Club of Chicago she rushed home showered, and dressed in a maroon-colored Louis Vuitton high waist asymmetric hem one-shoulder dress, matching Red Bottom heels and Louis Vuitton clutch purse, hair pulled up into a bun showing her neckline sitting on her chest just above her bosom sat a heart-shaped diamond necklace with a red ruby in the center. She followed the hostess as she showed her to her seat, where her guest awaited.

Once at the table the man waiting for her stood, he towered over her at 6'6 with a toned, Ballarino frame, angular cheekbones, warm brown eyes, and dark-haired Pompeo hairstyle. He wore a designer black tuxedo with a matching bowtie. He took her hand into his and kissed it, pulled her chair out for her, and once she was seated slid it in then returned to his seat opposite of her on the table. Veronica smiled. She caught the eye of a man sitting across from her, he had a brown complexion with slanted eyes that looked to be Black mixed with Asian he was staring at her. She was used to uncomfortable looks from men, she dismissed the action-focused back on her companion.

"Looking lovely as always D.A. Malone."

She smiled. "Thank you, and please just call me Veronica."

He bowed in approval. "Of course."

"Not that I don't appreciate every chance I can get to come down to Maple and Ash for some of the best steak dinners in the city, but what would someone like Mr. Tyler Takashi-Diaz want with a lowly civil servant such as myself?"

They both laughed. Before he could respond they were interrupted by the waiter, he placed two wine glasses on the table, then opened a bottle of red wine, poured it into the two glasses, and left the bottle on the table.

"I hope you don't mind I took the liberty of ordering the wine Component 'Demi-Lune' Saint Estephe 2016."

Veronica picked up her glass, placed it underneath her nose, and took in a whiff before placing the glass to her lips and taking a sip.

"Excellent choice Mr. Takashi-Diaz."

"I thought you may like it."

She placed her glass back on the table. "Now back to my original question, what is it that I can do for you?"

"For me?" He laughed. "No, it is I who wants to do for you."

She folded her hands together on the table in front of her. "You don't say, and what is it that you want to do for me?"

"Give you the thing in which you seek."

She raised an eyebrow, lips pursed. "Just like that huh?"

"Just like that."

"Strong words for even someone of your stature Mr. Takashi-Diaz."

"Just Tyler please, and before we go any further let me hear you say it."

"Say what?"

"The thing that you seek."

15

"You claim to know what it's in my heart, you tell me what it is that I seek."

"General Attorney position, say the word and it's yours."

She laughed. "Abracadabra huh?"

He joined in the laughter. "Not quite, but you're not as far off from the truth of that statement as you may think."

"Not only is nothing free in the world, but in Chicago, you tend to pay premium rates price for all services rendered sooner or later. . .often you pay on the former side."

"See you'll make an excellent General Attorney, you're sharp."

"You don't take me as a man that schmoozes, so show me some respect and tell me why it is that you want to do this "favor" for me?"

"Ha, I'm offended, not the type to schmooze well in any case before I answer your question tell me what it is that you know about me?"

She picked up her glass and took another sip before answering. "Not much, graduated from Stanford, not long after started a tech and computer chip manufacturing company. Sold that for billions, founded several app businesses, and sold them. Never married, no kids, and not much publicity about charities or fundraising but that doesn't mean that you don't give back, just may hate the limelight. No dirt that I could find, but just as the acts of charity don't mean that there isn't any there. No allegiances to any political parties in the early 2000's word is you helped a few local Republicans gain seats then in the next election you helped Dems and Independents."

"Not bad. Is that all?"

"You tell me, is there more?"

He smiled. "Veronica my dear, there's always more."

"I'm sure."

"It wasn't all Ivy League schools and country club living for me growing up, the son of a Mexican whore from Pilsen in the Lower West Side and father was a first-born American Chinese from Chinatown come up off of Argyle let me tell you it wasn't easy half chink, half spic I caught hell from both sides."

"I can imagine, what did your father do for a living?"

"He owned a restaurant, but in the basement, he ran a casino for the Tongs. Did that for forty years or so, thought I was going to follow in his footsteps he had a couple of the boys beat that out of me quick enough." He laughed. Veronica cracked an uneasy smile. He continued.

"No need to look alarmed, it helped me to build character I don't care if it's Englewood, Chinatown, Little Italy, or Boys Town you can't be soft living in Chicago my father often told me growing up that everyone on any given day is an eye blink away from an act of violence."

"That's harsh, what was your response to that?"

"Try not to blink."

They both laughed. "Colorful past Tyler."

"Everyone has skeletons, Veronica."

"Shit some of us have cemeteries."

His forehead wrinkled. "Do tell."

She picked up her menu and opened it. "Another story for another day Tyler."

"I'm going to hold you to that."

"I'm sure you will, so let's fast forward let's say everything is as you say it is and you get me in then what, what's my price? Let me tell you right now I'm not doing anything for the Tongs, Triads, or any other organized crime-"

He held up one hand causing her to pause. "Nothing like that, as I said that was my father's life, all I ask is that when I ask you to grant my request no questions asked."

Veronica placed her menu back on the table. "You will give me some time to consider this?"

He picked up his glass and swallowed all the liquid in one gulp. "Of course, you have until tomorrow evening around this time, I'll be having dinner with your opponent."

"Understandable, no allegiances, right?"

"Are you ready to order?"

***

Chapter Seven

Black held the door open for Stone as she walked into the homemade ice cream shop on 47th in Bronzeville he followed behind her as they made their way to the counter.

"You been here before?" Stone asked as she looked up at the menu, Stone was his friend with benefits they had been messing around for almost a year now, and still, nothing was official, he met her at the clinic working the Edwards case. She was 5'1, 145 lbs., light skin kissed by the sun was a golden brown, she wore glasses, normally wore her hair naturally blown out into an afro today it was pressed and straightened Black hadn't realized how long it was, it reached down her back.

"Yeah, been through once or twice on certain occasions."

"I bet, how many of your side pieces you done brought through here?"

Black laughed. "Man stop playing."

"Umm, hmm I bet this part of your routine with all ya Lil hoes."

"Whatever, only you can make getting ice cream into a hoe stomping grounds."

"Black, is that you?" A woman's voice said from behind. Black turned around to see where the voice came from when he spotted the woman, he froze in his tracks.

"You were saying, Black?" Stone said with her hands on her hips.

The woman rushed towards him and wrapped her arms around his neck in a hug. Black wrapped his arms around her waist hugging her back.

"I knew that was you!" They let go and took a long look at one another neither saying a word. Stone stepped up wedging herself in between the two, she extended her hand in a handshake. "Hi, I'm Stone and you are?"

She took Stone's hand in a handshake, her face turned flush red. "Oh, I'm sorry, I'm Morena, Black and I are old friends."

Morena Suarez was Black's ex-fiancé, he stared into her big brown eyes, her skin still looked a golden brown and smooth as ever, and her long, curly hair was no longer brunette and no longer curly it was straight and blonde. A perfect set of breasts sat snuggly in the tight-fitting track suit she wore, half-zipped open revealing the Nike logo of her sports bra she towered over Black almost six feet in height compared to his barely five and a half inches.

"What are you doing here Morena?" Black asked wrapping his arm around Stone's shoulder.

"I moved to this side of town, got tired of Logan Square."

Black laughed. "So, you move to Bronzeville?"

"Why not? It's the culture around here, nice Brownstones for a steal plus I feel closer to the people out here."

"Cool."

"What's been up with you, still the D.A.?"

"Nah, I'm doing something else now."

"What!? But you loved practicing law."

"Things change."

"They sure do!" She held up her hand to show the wedding band on her ring finger.

"You're married?"

"It's still new, but yes!"

Black hugged her again. "Congratulations, I'm happy for you."

"Yeah congratulations, we should celebrate you and your new boo are coming over to Black's for dinner and I will not accept no for an answer," Stone said as a matter of fact.

"I don't know if that's a good idea Stone," Morena said taking a step back.

"Bullshit, it's a done deal, dinner, tonight it'll be fun." Stone insisted.

"Sure, come on over, I'd love to meet him," Black said eagerly encouraging her to come over for dinner.

"Morena, you didn't order for me, did you? I didn't mean to take so long in the bathroom." A woman's voice shouted. Black recognized the voice, and when she rounded the corner and came into view Black was once again shocked. The woman froze in her tracks staring at the group. "Black!"

"Teresa, you're here too?" Teresa, another ex-fiancé he'd introduced the two through a tragic happenstance he hadn't expected that they'd remain friends. Teresa still looked good.

"Uh, yeah." She responded.

"I didn't know that you two kept in contact."

Teresa locked her hand into Morena's. "Black we've done more than keep in contact, we're married."

***

21

Chapter Eight

Black pulled up in front of the church at 9536 S. Minnick that would soon serve as his base of operations, only gone a week or so Parker had already shown great progress with cleaning up the property. He shifted the car into park and stepped out, closing the door he leaned on the hood of the car and looked up at the building. In bright red letters were the words "Love Detective Agency" across the front of the building. He smiled to himself. "Not bad." He said to himself then made his way around the car, up the stairs, and through the open front door of the building. Gone were the litter, rodents, and decaying floor. A handful of workers moved about the property nailing, sanding, and painting. He ignored the workers and continued through the building looking for Parker.

Making his way into the kitchen he found Parker lying on the floor working on the plumbing for the sink. Parker stands up and nods at Black, and grabs a bottle of water from the kitchen counter.

"How did the meeting go with the detectives?" Parker asked in between swigs.

Black shook his head. "It was a little funky the way it went down, but I told them no."

"No, why?"

"I don't see these cases being connected."

"Who gives a fuck, that's a guaranteed check it's through the government you shouldn't have turned down the case without hollering at me first."

"I get it, Parker you're anxious to get cracking but trust me this case. . .it ain't it."

"No, you don't get it I'm not anxious and I ain't a worker we're partners just put me in the loop before you get to turning shit down from now on can you do that for me, Mr. Love?"

Black chuckled. "Yeah, I can do that, speaking of Mr. Love I'm digging the name of the business."

Parker smirked. "Yeah, I figured you would."

"Man, guess who I ran into yesterday at Shawn Michelle's ice cream shop, I was with the little chick I told you about Stone."

"Who?"

"Morena."

"The Hispanic chick you was going marry?"

Black smiled. "Yeah, and guess who she was with?"

"Who?"

"Teresa."

Parker laughed. "The other chick you were going marry?"

Black shook his head in defeat. "Yep and the broads got married."

"To each other?"

"Hell yeah."

"You bull-shitting."

"Fucked me up."

Parker burst into a fit of laughter. "So, you're telling me your new dip, what's her name Stone, was in the spot with you and two of your exes all together?"

"Man, hell yeah."

"Awkward as hell."

"Nigga I was going through it how you think I felt."

Parker laughed again. "What happened?"

"Stone not knowing what's going on, made the shit worst?"

"I know you told me shorty borderline hood, don't tell me little mama started wilding out?"

"Nah, worst."

"What could be worse than that?"

"Man, she invited them over to dinner at my place."

Parker laughed. "Man, what you say?"

"I said yeah."

"Nigga what made you do something like that?"

"It was before I knew they were married, I already said yeah so I had to flow with it."

Parker shook his head. "Only you could end up in a situation like this how did Stone play it when you told her the whole story?"

"Surprisingly, she didn't trip."

Parker raised an eyebrow. "She was cool with it?"

"Fucked me up too, I mean technically we aren't dating so she can't trip."

"Man quit playing when has that ever mattered to a woman?'

"I hear you; I need a favor though."

"What's up?"

"Man, I need a buffer between me, and all these damn women slide through to the dinner."

"Nuh-uh, my brother you're on your own I ain't getting in the middle of your soap opera shit."

"Come on bro it ain't even like that."

"Even worse I'm not getting in the middle of your orgy shit either."

Black laughed. "So, you just going leave a brother hanging?"

Parker jumped up on the counter and sat down. "Man, fuck it I'll come through on one condition."

"What's that?"

"You can't be the only one there with all that pussy, I got to bring a date."

Black laughed. "Man stop I ain't going be there with all that pussy, you going to come or what?"

"I can bring a date?"

"Man, yeah I don't care, who are you planning on bringing anyway?"

Parker jumped down from the counter. "Man, this thick little chick I met yesterday she cute as hell she's a-"

Before he could complete his sentence, he stopped short when Trigger entered the kitchen from the stairs behind them. Black turned his attention to Trigger, they stared at one another neither saying a word. Parker nodded at Black. "I'll holler at you later Black; Trigger I'll see you tomorrow I'm done for the day."

Trigger nodded, still not speaking until he left the kitchen. Trigger was his off-and-on lover, Trigger was five and a half feet of toned, mocha, sexiness. Silk and steel. Sexy and smooth as silk yet looking at her body it was obvious, she worked out she looked to be as solid as steel, in a feminine way that is. She wore her hair naturally; it had a curly bounce to it that came down and stopped at the bottom of her ears. Her eyes held a slight slant to them as if mixed with Asian, although she often got upset by the question if she were mixed, which she wasn't. Nice B cups, and cuff able derriere, with a smile that made hearts skip beats she was 145 lbs. of raw sex appeal. She was also a contractor. Parker hired her to refurbish the building. "You just going stare at me Black or are you going to speak?"

Black cleared his throat. "How are you doing Trigger?"

"I'm good, no hug?"

Black stepped closer with his arms open and she stepped into them. He took in her scent of lavender body spray the pheromones activated immediately, and the bulge in his pants pressed against her. They stepped apart. She smiled up at him. "Everything been good?"

"Yeah, just got back in town."

"Yeah, I know, Pops told me."

"He did, did he, he didn't tell me you would be the one doing the repairs around here."

"That's not a problem, is it?"

"No, why would it?"

She shrugged her shoulders. "Just asking."

"How was your trip?"

"I don't want to talk about it."

"That bad huh?"

"The place looks great so far."

"It's a lot of space what are you going to do with all of it?"

"I don't know, we're kind of taking it one step at a time know what I mean?"

She shook her head yes. "I do, I'm proud of you Black."

"Thanks, it's all a process, right?"

"Yes, sir." She leaned in and kissed him on the lips. "You know I miss you right?"

He took her into a hug. "I miss you too."

***

Chapter Nine

"Mama, somebody at the door!" Sage, Stone's youngest daughter yelled. Trigger entered the living room wearing a wife beater and boy shorts.

"Turn that game off and get ready for bed."

Sage did as her mother said she got up from the couch, and turned off the television and game console. Stone made her way to the door, standing on her toes looked through the peephole.

"Who is it?" She yelled through the door.

"Julius!" A familiar voice yelled back through the door. She took a step back from the door, placed her hands on her hips, and her lips twisted into a snarl she turned and faced her daughter. "Sleep in the room tonight, your sister is spending the night at a friend's."

Sage stared back with pleading eyes. "Mama!"

Stone rolled her eyes. "Fine." She opened the door and stepped to the side to allow him to enter, as he stepped inside Sage rushed him and jumped into his arms.

"Daddy, daddy, daddy!"

He held her close in a hug. "Hey, baby!"

"I missed you so much, daddy!"

"I missed you too baby, where's your brother and sister?"

"They all had stuff to do, they are gone you staying here tonight daddy?"

Julius placed her on the floor. "I don't know baby, that's up to your mama."

"No, he is not, you saw him now do what I told you."

Sage pouted. Wrapped her arms around her father's waist. "Love you daddy, hope you're still here when I go to school in the morning."

"Love you to pumpkin."

She let go and ran off to her sister's bedroom closing the door behind her. Stone folded her arms across her chest. "What do you want Julius?"

"A man can't come to see his family?"

She laughed. "Boy please we've never been a family and it's late as hell to be just popping up at my shit what if I would've had a man here?"

He looked over her shoulder toward her bedroom. "Do you?"

She rolled her neck. "And if I do?"

Julius smirked. "You would have to go back there and tell your company it's time to leave."

She laughed. "Nigga please, this-"

"I didn't come here for that, is it a nigga back there or what?" He attempted to push past her, but she held both hands up pushing him back. She pointed a finger in his face.

"You don't just walk through here like you pay bills or some shit, no there's no one here and if it were, he would be talking to you, not me."

Julius laughed. "Same old shit-talking Stone."

Stone smirked. "Same old bull shit ass Julius."

"I need a place to stay for a while."

"If you ain't notice this ain't no Ramada Inn."

"Get off that shit Stone, I'm serious."

"And I look like I'm playing? We ain't seen you in years and you pop up out of the blue? How the hell do you know where I stay anyway?"

"Ran into your father back home in Ohio, the old man still playing with the best of em don't have as many girls on the stroll as he had when I first met you but his pimp hand still strong."

"Umm, hmm going have to talk to him about some shit."

"Are you going to let me stay or what?"

"No, there's no room, Sapphire has her room cause she's a teenage girl, the other kids sleep out here on the let-out couches."

"What's wrong with your room?"

"Be for real, you ain't sleeping with me."

"I am for real; shit we have four kids together you don't have nothing I ain't seen."

"That's the point, you won't be seeing it anymore."

"I would get a room, but I need to lay low for a while can't leave a paper trail, I have some serious people with long money and a long reach looking for me."

She shook her head. "Same old Julius you took the wrong people's shit this time in that case you definitely can't stay here don't need drama showing up at my door if you don't care about what happens to our kids I do."

"How are you going say some shit like that? You know damn well I care about what happens to our kids."

"Not being in their lives and providing for them financially is how I can say that." She walked over to the door and opened it.

He stared back with pleading eyes. She looked him up and down, he hadn't changed much physically. Towering over her at almost six and a half feet his dreads tied back into a ponytail, he had tattoos running down both sides of his arms and the left side of his neck, skin tone a rough dark black with his beard hanging long from his face. She closed the door.

"You can stay one night, sleep on the couch I want you gone before Sage goes to school in the morning don't need you getting her hopes up and if you try to creep back to my room in the middle of the night, I will shoot you, call the police and tell em you broke in." She walked past him into her room and closed the door.

***

Chapter Ten

The school bus moved along the highway in Aurora, IL getting off at an exit not too far from where he picked up the all-girl volleyball team from Rosary High School driving down a two-lane road the cackling pre-teen girl hadn't paid any attention that the driver wasn't the driver that dropped them off at their game, let alone that they had gotten off of the highway and were headed towards a desolate area. The bus pulled into an abandoned parking lot and parked, the driver turned the engine off and faced the girls.

"Quiet down girls!" He yelled towards the back of the bus. The girls ignored him continuing with their chatter and laughter. "I said shut the hell up!" He yelled louder this time, and the conversation abruptly halted. He smiled. "Now, sorry I had to yell but I'm having issues with the bus, I called for another bus to pick you guys up it may be a while I suggest you all get off of the bus and stretch your legs." He opened the door, and the girls began piling out. Positioned next to the bus was a cargo van, once all the girls were off the bus, he closed the bus door and grabbed the girl closest to him before any of them realized what was going on, he had already cut her twice underneath her ribcage. The girls all screamed and ran towards the bus clamoring to get inside.

"Nobody runs or I'm going to slit her throat." He said as he held her tighter and placed the bloody blade across her neck."

The girls began crying and pleading with the driver. He ignored their pleas.

"You there, slide that door open and the lot of you begin piling in, come on now I'm not going to ask twice do as your told."

The girl nearest to the van did as she was told and the girls one by one began climbing in until only the driver and the girl he stabbed remained, he shoved her to the ground. "Now you, get in let's go on your feet girl!" He demanded as he watched her blood seep into the dirt while she struggled to her feet. She limped towards the van slowly, looking back at her attacker.

"What are you doing, stop looking at me and get in the van."

She took off running as fast as she could clutching her side and screaming. She didn't get far, he grabbed her by her hair and pulled her towards him covering her mouth with one hand and running the knife across her neck with the other. When there was no more fight left in her he threw her across his shoulder and carried her back to the van. He tossed her in the back with the rest of the girls.

"That's what's coming to anyone else who takes it upon themselves to not do as I say and run." He slammed the door closed as the girls bawled their eyes out.

***

Chapter Eleven

After driving the hour from Aurora to Gary, IN he was back at his killing floor, that's what he called it he had the girls bound, blindfolded, and gagged secured in separate rooms all but one, he had her tied to the table with the dead girl near his feet on the floor of the warehouse.

"What's wrong with people? Huh?" He asked the girl tied to the table with a gag in her mouth, she stared back tears falling from her eyes.

"You would think the New Trier girls would have been enough for them to do something, but I guess they just didn't matter. . .you just don't matter."

He shook his head woefully and broke out into song. "It's been too hard living, but I'm afraid to die 'Cause I don't know what's up there, beyond the sky It's been a long, a long time coming But I know a change gonna come, oh yes it will." He pressed down on her forehead to hold her head in place and ran the blade across her neck, he watched as the fight left her body. Placed the bloody blade on the table and picked up an electric jigsaw and powered it on starting with her left arm he went to work.

***

Chapter Twelve

No one paid any particular attention to the pale teenage girl as she wandered into the lobby area of the Amita Health Mercy Medical Center in Aurora, Il one of the missing girls from Rosary High school she had only been gone under 24 hours yet with the loss of blood drained from her body her skin tone looked blanched. Staggering a few more feet before passing out, people standing near gasped as a nurse pushed through the crowd and cradled the girl's head in her lap.

"Get a bed!" The nurse yelled out to no one in particular. It wasn't long before two nurses emerged pushing a bed, the two easily lifted the girl and placed her on the bed. The original nurse now to her feet standing near the bed placed her hands on the girl's eyelids gently opening them. "What's your name?" She let her eyes go and they closed, the girl was unresponsive. The nurse noticed blood seeping through her shirt. She removed a pair of scissors from the pocket of her scrubs jacket and beginning at the bottom of the girl's shirt she began cutting. The nurse gasped. Carved into her stomach were the words: Ning Cai, Lucifer & Ehrich Weiss- Black Love XOXO. "Oh my, we have to get her to an emergency room!"

***

Chapter Thirteen

Veronica wore an all-white blazer and pants smart-looking business suit, and heels, hair pulled up into a bun. A bit over-dressed for the evening, but this was more of a networking event than it was a social gathering. She moved seamlessly through the room of thirty or more people in the luxury sky box at Soldier's Field stadium, the Bears were playing the Packers, but no one paid attention to the game. A mixture of Hors d'oeuvres and finger foods such as mini sandwiches and a tray of hot wings were being served as others either sipped flutes filled with champagne or tossed back glasses of beer. Veronica held on to Tyler's arm as he moved from one part of the room to the next introducing her to different political donors.

She whispered into Tyler's ear. "I thought being the D.A. I knew a good portion of the heavy hitters in Chicago, you've proven me wrong."

Tyler laughed. "I don't know how heavy they are, but at the very least they are good people to be acquainted with." They found themselves face to face with a woman evenly tanned, toned, average-height brunette with freckles speckling her nose and underneath her eyes. Veronica smiled, then reached out her hand and shook hands with the potential donor. Tyler made the introductions. "Allow me to introduce the next Attorney General, Ms. Veronica Malone, Veronica I want you to meet a very important lady to me Erica Vice."

Veronica laughed. "Is that right, well nice to meet you, Ms. Vice." Before releasing her hand from the handshake Veronica couldn't help but notice the scar running down her forearm from where her arm bends stretching down the length of her arm stopping just before her wrist. She looked up and her eyes met Erica's, they both silently acknowledged the scar, and neither said a word. They both smiled.

Tyler spoke. "Erica just recently returned from Ontario, Canada she worked in part with the Executive Coordinator for the Organizing and Electoral Campaigns Department of the Planned Parenthood organization."

"It sounds as if you have some experience with campaign raising?"

Erica smiled. "I do what I can, I trust Tyler and if he says trust you, then a donation is the least I could do, I do have a curiosity you could help me with though."

"And that would be?"

"I was studying your background before I came to this soi·rée I am so fascinated with true crime mysteries."

Veronica raised an eyebrow but didn't interrupt. Erica continued. "I know you had no direct involvement with the missing girls from a few years ago but I was intrigued to see that your coworker was the Blue fellow who found the girls. I don't mean to come off as some crazed prison groupie, but I'd love to meet him, and pick his brain are you, two colleagues?"

Veronica's forehead wrinkled. "Blue? Prison groupie, I'm sorry but I am lost."

Erica laughed. "Que je suis bête…silly me, I must have my colors mixed up it is an unusual name he helped to find the colored girls."

Veronica cleared her throat. "The African American girls, yes and his name is Black, yes we are acquaintances why do you ask?"

"As I said, not to come off as a groupie people like that intrigue me how they get into the mind of people like that you know the whole cat and mouse hunter and prey game."

Veronica took a swallow from her glass. "I'll get your information from Tyler, have Black reach out to you I'm sure he'd love to meet you."

"Fantastic."

Veronica smiled- locked eyes with a man across the room, he wore a Chicago Bears jersey and ball cap. Just under average height, and looked to be mixed with Black and Asian. "He looks familiar," Veronica said once again wrapping her arm around Tyler's.

"What was that?" Tyler asked as he placed his hand on top of hers.

Veronica looked back up and the man was gone. "Never mind." The duo moved on to the next guest.

***

Chapter Fourteen

Stone stepped from Black's bedroom into his living room wearing a turquoise-colored tube chemise strapless dress and matching pumps her fingernails were painted dark mahogany. She smiled at Black as he placed a platter of crackers and spread-able cheeses: port wine, cheddar, and herb garden on a table in front of his exes Teresa and Morena. He wore a black V-neck sweater with matching silk slacks and hard-bottom dress shoes. Eminem and Gwen Stefani's King's Never Die played in the background. There was a knock at the door. "Get the wine for me," Black said directed towards Stone as he made his way to the door and opened it. Standing on the other side of the door was Parker, Black ushered him in leaving the door partially open.

"I thought you were bringing someone?"

"I did, she ran back to her car, she forgot her phone." Just as he finished his sentence there was a tap at the door and the door was gently nudged open standing on the other side of the door was Veronica. Black stared blankly. She extended her hand.

"Hi, I'm Veronica Malone."

Black took her hand into his. "Black, nice to meet you." He closed the door after she was inside.

"I told you she was bad, didn't I?" Parker said to Black laughing.

Veronica blushed. "Boy stop."

"Shit you are, and she's a lawyer too brains and beauty you two ever crossed paths?"

"Damn it! Will one of you men help me with this bottle, I got the damn corkscrew stuck in the bottle?" Stone yelled out interrupting their conversation.

"Don't worry about it I'll take care of that for you, sister," Parker says as he rushes off to help to leave Black and Veronica alone.

"Why didn't you tell me you were fucking around with my boy?"

"Excuse me? You aren't my man and besides I didn't know you two knew each other he didn't tell me the friend's name just told me about the funny situation with your exes and the night might be entertaining. He didn't tell you I was coming?"

"Yes, but didn't say who was coming."

"Well, it should go without saying that you don't need to mention us ever messing around."

"Is that so? It's a good thing you did say something be-because I have every intention of saying something it's my guy, my best friend we don't hold shit like this from each other."

"Why? You get off on awkward situations Black? Two of your exes are now married, your new chick is serving wine and now throw into the mix you once fucked your best friend's date that's a little too interesting of an evening for me, keep your mouth shut lest I remind you, you owe me multiple favors."

"If I keep quiet about this, after tonight you are going to break it off with Parker, right?"

"Again, not your business Black."

***

Chapter Fifteen

Stewart and Jones turn the corner onto Wentworth cruising down the one-way street, they let their eyes scan the block every other home is boarded up and those that aren't boarded are a patch of land where a home used to stand. Roseland, a mostly all-black middle-class community had its share of crime, mostly gang-related but for the most part, it was a community of working-class church people. Jones sat behind the wheel he pulled behind a Tahoe and parked upon reaching their destination. He turned the car off and grabbed the door handle.

"Let me take this one alone," Stewart said to her partner.

He closed the door and turned to her. "Are you serious, why?"

"He's an old man, and you tend to rub people the wrong way let me talk to him I have more of a soft touch."

"You need back up you can't go in there alone; besides, I'll just listen I won't say a word."

Her forehead wrinkled. "He's a senior citizen I'm pretty sure I won't need back-up and when have you ever not said anything?"

Jones stared her down for several seconds. "Fine, ten minutes then I'm coming in."

She smiled. "Don't pout, we need some information on this Love guy according to his former colleagues in the district attorney's office he didn't have many friends, only living relative that they know of in the city…a Pope Love, everyone calls him Pops retired postman almost twenty years now, ex-military served in

Vietnam, no criminal record, no record of a wife on file, lives alone."

"Why talk to this guy at all, I doubt he can help with the investigation."

"You peg Love for these missing girls' cases, right?"

"Evidence points that way."

"Let's get some insight into how those around him see him try to build a profile, trust me."

***

Chapter Sixteen

"Dinner was pretty good," Parker says as he flops down on the couch next to Veronica, removes a pre-rolled marijuana blunt from his pocket places it between his lips and lights it. Veronica shifts in her seat so that she is facing him.

"You do know that I am an officer of the court, don't you?"

He took a long pull, then blew the smoke in her face. "Arrest me then."

She pulled the blunt from his mouth, turned it, placed it in her mouth, and took a pull. She blew smoke into his face. "First of all, I don't arrest people, that's the police job…I will charge your ass though when they bring you in."

The room erupted into laughter. She offered the joint to Black who was sitting across from her, he took it and passed it to Stone, who was sitting on his lap. She took it and drew in a mouthful of smoke.

"You know Black I met this woman, at my campaign party earlier today she was fascinated with you and said she wanted to meet you," Veronica said as she played with Parker's beard.

"Let me find out you around here with groupies and shit." Stone said as the room started laughing.

"What's her name?" Black asked directed towards Veronica.

"Erica Vice she raises funds says she's out of Ontario, Canada."

"Never heard of her."

"I'll pass her your info; she seems to have deep pockets and political connections and might be a good person to know."

"Any new cases you are working on Black?" Morena asked as she took the blunt from Stone and took a pull.

"Can't say that I am."

"What are you talking about Black, aren't you going to work the New Trier case?" Veronica asked as she leaned back and rested her frame against Parker's.

Black picked up his glass of wine and emptied it in one swallow. "I never said yes."

"That's that bullshit I was talking about," Parker said as the blunt made it's way back to him.

"Why the reluctance to take the case, Black?" Morena asked as she ran her finger underneath Teresa's chin.

"A lot of stuff doesn't sit right with me."

"Like what, money?" Parker asked, once again passing the now dwindling blunt back to Veronica for a second pull.

Black laughed. "Money has nothing to do with it."

"Shid, from where I sit money has damn near everything to do with it," Parker said then laughed.

Black continued. "Money ain't got shit to do with it bruh, I ain't in it for the money I want to help people for real."

"Well Black, aren't those missing New Trier girls' people too?" Morena asked joining back into the conversation.

"Yes, they are, but they have resources and are more than likely the offspring of folks that got money and influence they don't need me caping for them."

Stone shifted in his lap so that she could get a better view of his face. "So, you're telling me that you don't want to help find those girls cause they're white and they're people got money?"

Black laughed. "I see what you guys are trying to do and it's not going to work."

"I don't know what you are talking about bruh," Parker said, as he ran his hands up and down Veronica's thighs.

"They know what I'm talking about, the shit just ain't fair, when I was looking for them girls from the South Side ain't nobody gives a fuck, I mean shit was quiet they damn near was acting like I was making the shit up about the girls coming up missing. But as soon as little white girls start disappearing in big numbers, they pull out all the stops, look online that shit is everywhere. Can't turn on the TV or the radio without hearing an ad about a reward for information."

Morena smirked. "I'm sure you're exaggerating Black."

"The hell I am, just ask Veronica, she'll tell you."

Everyone's eyes shifted toward Veronica. She cleared her throat. "Although Black is right in some respects, that's not what's important here."

"What's important then?" Stone asked as she took what was remaining of the blunt from Veronica.

"That we bring children home safely, I don't care if they're white, black, Asian or hybrids they're innocent and have nothing to do with the stupid political games that adults play."

Black grimaced at the remark. "Why don't you tell them what the department is doing to help facilitate their return."

Veronica rolled her eyes at Black before answering the question. "Resources will be allocated to help pay for overtime for the detectives on the case, volunteer search parties are also being paid a stipend for their participation, and funds were set aside for Black and his team. We've also assembled a separate task force specifically for this case until someone is captured."

"And you guys didn't do any of this for the black girls that were missing?" Stone asked staring in shock.

"Unfortunately, not, the funds just weren't available at the time," Veronica responded defensively.

Black laughed. "Ain't that convenient when the Black girls were missing there was no money to be found, now that the privileged white chirren are in need money and resources are miraculously allocated."

Morena chimed back in. "Wait Black, this could be a good thing right, let's say you do help find the girls, once this is all done then you can use the task force and the same money for the media coverage for the New Trier girls for the girls on the south side."

"That shit doesn't work that way, does it, Veronica?" Black said placing Veronica back into the hot seat.

"Once again, unfortunately not, more than likely after this case is closed rather the girls are found or not the task force will be disassembled, and any remaining funds will be distributed as the command chief sees fit and I doubt they'll give it to the missing person department in the 4th district."

"That's fucked up." Stone said laying her head back onto Black's chest. "I see why you don't want to do it."

"Shit I don't," Parker said putting his two cents into the conversation. "Look nigga, if we take the money and help or we don't the money still getting spent and they still ain't going give niggas shit on the southside might as well get ours and get some free publicity for the business at the same time especially if we the ones that find them, little girls whatever they offering to pay us you tell them to double that shit."

"Keeping it real, my heart just ain't it, I ain't doubting myself but y'all don't know the shit I just went through in Nigeria, then to come home and this shit is dumped in my lap as soon as I step off the plane. Don't get me wrong I understand what everyone is saying, believe me, I do, I just feel like a big ass hypocrite to be a part of a super team for white folks trying to make them whole again, and the same wasn't done for my people, don't those black girls families deserve to be whole again?" Black said to a now quiet room.

Teresa who had yet to voice her opinion broke the silence. "All I know is that no one was going to fight for me when I had my incident in Danville, you were the only one who would fight for me set your pride to the side, and do the right thing Black fight for those girls."

***

Chapter Seventeen

Stewart sat across from Pops in his living room, and they both sipped from bottles of IceHouse beer. Sparkle, his all-white Pitbull lye on the floor near his feet.

"What can I do for you detective?"

"Just need you to answer a few questions about your son."

"Yeah, is he suspected of doing something?"

She flashed a smile. "Of course, not sir."

"That's good to know, if that's the case why not ask him, being the former district attorney, he has a relationship with the police."

She took another sip from her bottle. "I'm aware of that, but we would like to know what the people closest to him have to say to get a clearer picture of his personality."

"And you need to know this why?"

"We want him to be a part of a task force to find those missing New Trier girls, I'm sure you've heard about it."

"Um, hmm."

She cleared her throat. "We just need to make sure that Black is the right man for the job."

"Oh, is that all? A smile crept across Pops face. "Well, if that's all, yes, he's the right person."

Stewart laughed. "I'm afraid it's not that simple."

"Don't bullshit me detective why are you here?"

"Did Black talk to you about a Charles Tyner or Avery Gillian?"

"No, everything that I know I found out on the internet or the news, Black doesn't talk to me about cases."

"I find that hard to believe Mr. Love."

"Believe what you like child I'm telling you what it is."

"I see, and what about a Parker Harris?"

"What about him?"

"What can you tell me of him and Black's relationship?"

"The fact that you ask tells me that you already know."

She smiled. "Childhood friends."

"Umm, hmm."

"Does Black make it a habit of making friends with known felons?"

"Again, that would be a question you would have to ask Black."

"Just a few more questions-"

Pops stood to his feet; Sparkle stood as well. "I'm sorry detective, I don't see how I can help you, I'm about to start my show Judge Mathis is about to come on now you're welcome to join me, but they'll be no more talk of my son."

Stewart stood to her feet, and extended her hand to Pops, he took it in a firm shake. "Thank you for your time, and the beer."

"You be safe out there."

She left the home beer still in hand, took a swallow finished it off, and climbed back into the car behind the wheel.

"He give you anything?" Her partner asked as he took the beer bottle and tossed it out into the street.

"No." Before she pulled off, she looked back up at the house to find Pops standing in the doorway watching her.

***

Shaunte stood alone waiting at the L station on the Argyle red line, she had gotten off work later than her regular time so the usual crowd that is out waiting to go home had already gone. She normally wouldn't have been afraid, but tonight seemed eerily quiet. She didn't like the quiet, or the cold it reminded her of time spent as a captive with the other three girls locked in the walk-in cooler a few years ago. She felt silly being afraid, there was no way that they would come back for her, her parents kept in contact with the police and as far as anyone knew the people that had abducted her were on the run, there was no way that they would return to Chicago. To take her mind off being afraid she placed her earbuds into her ears and turned her music on her phone. She stepped closer to the tracks and looked down the tracks to see if she could see the lights from a train coming. As she took a step back, a hand was placed over her mouth, and she was picked up off her feet and carried towards the stairs. She struggled with her abductor; screams muffled she dropped her phone during the scuffle she fought harder as she saw the train approaching, as the abductor whispered in her ear. "You keep fighting me, I'll throw your ass in front of the train."

Shaunte stopped struggling as the abductor ran down the stairs to a waiting truck with the tailgate open, she was tossed into the truck before she had the chance to try and fight again, she was struck in the chest with a stun gun. The kidnapper climbed in behind her and closed the door, tied her arms and legs with rope, and climbed over the seats until she reached the driver's seat, started the truck, and pulled off.

The train screeches to a stop and the doors open, passengers flood the platform exiting the train, and just as the doors begin to close the last passenger steps out, pauses, looks down at his feet, and picks up an iPhone, he runs his thumb across the screen attempting to open the phone, but the screen is locked. He looks around the platform to find that he is alone, he shoves the phone into his pocket and hustles down the stairs.

***

Chapter Eighteen

The phone rang waking Black from his sleep, he reached over and grabbed it off the stand next to his bed, he ran his thumb across the screen the phone unlocked. It was a text message. He looked over at Stone, lying next to him in his bed. She had spent a night, it was the first time that she had done so since them knowing one another Black didn't know how to take that, was their relationship changing in some way that he was unaware of, did she just want a change of scenery or was she edging towards getting serious? He climbed from bed and grabbed the pants he had on the day before from the floor slid them on and grabbed his shirt from the floor, he looked up to find Stone looking at him.

"Where are you going?" She asked as she propped herself up on her elbows.

He leaned down and placed a kiss on her lips. "Go back to bed, I won't be long, have a thing to do."

She rolled her eyes and rolled back over, turning her back to him. "Don't be long, I didn't spend the night to sleep alone."

He didn't respond, he grabbed his keys from the dresser and left the room. It wasn't long before he was on the road and headed towards Bronzeville he found a place to park and began walking to the Lakefront Trail. When he got the text, he was surprised, although he wasn't in a relationship with Stone it was borderline wrong to leave her to go to a meet-up, he couldn't tell her no, he never could. After a brisk walk along the trail, he felt like a teenage boy almost didn't know where to find the words when he found himself alone with her for the first time since Danville.

"What's up Black, thank you for coming."

Black stared blankly. "What's up with you, what's on your mind, Teresa?"

***

After making sure that Teresa was in her car and safely on her way, he spotted a familiar face watching. Black didn't know whether to feel excited to see the man or sad. They worked together once if you could call it that. The man was about an inch shorter than Black and had the same weight and build, hair cut short, skin just as dark as Black's, and with slanted eyes, a Black/Asian hybrid. Helped Black with the missing black girls from the cannibal case. He wanted Black to find his sister, but they never did. Black knew this wasn't a coincidence he pops back up into his life after he joins the New Trier task force.

"Long time no see Crishan, thought you probably went back to Malaysia."

"Can't unfinished business here."

"What can I do for you?"

"Nothing, just being cordial."

"Bullshit."

"Make of it what you want."

"Well, I feel like I owe you one, you need me for something reach out."

Crishan nodded that he understood. Black nodded back, got into his car, and pulled off.

***

Chapter Nineteen

Black reluctantly agreed to work with the special unit looking for the New Trier girls, he tried to push down his reservations about working the case, but it was hard, especially being stationed out of the Broadway Armory Park seeing all the volunteers and other officers devoting so much time and attention to the case he felt like a sellout. He had spent the better part of the day interviewing potential witnesses, with the reward being offered they were flooded with false leads, and he was doing his part to help weed out the timewasters so that the detectives could focus their time on the more solid leads.

He sat across from what had to have been the fiftieth witness, he was zoning in and out his mind was focused on the latest victim that had been dropped at the hospital with his name carved into her torso, she hadn't survived. He knew that it was targeted towards him, he just didn't know why, if he could get the why, he had no doubt he would get the who. As he jotted down a few notes about what the potential witness said, he stopped when he heard a commotion coming from behind him. He turned to find Parker standing toe to toe with Jones. He stood and rushed over to intervene.

"What's going on here?" Black demanded as he pushed Parker behind him.

"He isn't authorized to be in here."

"The hell are you talking about Jones, you know damn well he works with me, and two: every swinging dick with in a thousand miles of New Trier is walking in here off the street to give information and claim that cash reward, I've been here for hours, and this is the first I've seen you or any other officer deny anyone access."

"Look, Love, you or no one else is coming in here and telling me how to run things."

"Don't worry about it, we're out of here and when the D.A. and your Captain ask me why I quit the investigation I'll let them know it was at your behest."

"Just keep your boy in line and out of our way."

"I'll show you who's the boy." Parker said as he pushed past Black and squared up with Jones."

"You give him the same respect you give anyone else in here or we leave right here, right now!"

Jones didn't respond verbally, he stared at the two men for several seconds. "Just stay out of my way!" He walked past both Black and Parker and went outside.

***

Chapter Twenty

The maroon-colored 2000 Land Rover with tinted windows pulled into the parking lot of the Broadway Armory Park, powered off the vehicle looked at himself in the rearview mirror, Adjusted the device on his military-style vest that he wore, and stepped from the vehicle. He carried a folder with him, he walked into the building and towards the hall that was rented by the police and the special task force that was conducting the manhunt for the missing girls and the abductor. He opened the doors to the hall and was floored to find so many people there. He began to appear to be speaking to himself.

"You see this? Let me see if I had to guess, we have what looks like CPD, a gaggle of detectives: Chicago homicide, missing persons, maybe some Northfield, IL detectives, might even be some FEDS working this one." He laughed. "Over there they look like civilians, don't you just love how the community comes out and helps one another. Oh shit, how did they get him involved? I know you remember him, overnight internet sensation Black Love."

"Excuse me, sir, can I help you?" A voice says from behind the man.

He turns and faces the stranger. "Yes, I'm looking for the detective in charge of the New Trier investigation."

"And you are?"

"Looking for the detective in charge."

The two had a brief stare-off. "I'm detective Jones and your name would be?"

"Salt, Jon Salt, and I have some information that can help the case."

Jones began walking away. "Follow me." Salt followed behind until they were at a fold-up table and two fold-up chairs sitting next to one another. The table was scattered with papers and photos. "Cop a squat." Jones insisted.

Salt shook his head no. "I'll stand."

Jones folded his arms across his chest. "What's this information?" Salt offered the folder to Jones he took it, opened it, and began reading. "This is from a few years ago."

"It is."

"How are these two cases connected?"

"The New Trier girls are teenaged girls; my little girl was a teenaged girl."

Jones closed the folder and handed it back to Salt. "Sir, I understand your frustration and I sympathize with your loss, but this case has nothing to do with our case, did you reach out to the detective in charge of your case?"

"I did, he's moved on."

"I'm sorry, that's an unfortunate fact but sometimes cases run cold."

"And it's off to the next, screw my family, the pain that my wife and I share!"

"Sir, calm down, there's no need to raise your voice."

Salt stared into Jones' eyes. "No sir, you get riled up about finding my little girl like your fired up about finding the white girls."

"I resent the accusation, I put my heart into all of my cases I don't give a damn what they look like."

Salt laughed. Raising his voice once more. "You and I both know that's a got damn lie, if my little girl was blue-eyed and blonde, they would have found her by now. When the half-ass investigation into finding her was still ongoing I saw none of this shit. I mean look around here you would think the President's daughter was kidnapped."

"Sir I'm going to have to ask you to leave, there's nothing more we can do for you."

"I'm not going any place; you haven't done anything yet."

"Which may be a good thing, I'm homicide police so there's still some hope for finding your little girl, if I get involved, it's too late."

"Don't try to twist this around, I want justice and I want it now!" Salt yelled as everyone stopped what they were doing and faced the two.

"I'm going to ask you one last time to leave peacefully, next time I'm taking you out in cuffs."

Salt stepped closer to Jones so that they were nose to nose. "The hell you are, you can't intimidate me."

Before it escalated any further, Parker stepped up and intervened. "Excuse me detective Jones let me see if I can help my man. He extended his hand out to Salt. "I'm Parker, what can I do to help you?"

"I got this, con…um, uh Parker."

Salt stared down at Parker's hand not accepting his offer of a handshake. "And what do you do around here Parker?"

"I'm a part of Love Detective Agency we were hired as consultants, if you just come with me, I give you my word we will hear you out and try to come up with a plan."

Salt nodded in agreement. Parker turned and headed back to an area of the hall where he and Black were stationed. Black stood to his feet and reached out his hand to shake Salt's hand.

"I'm Black and you are?"

Salt stared at his hand for several seconds before accepting it in a handshake.

"Jon, Jon Salt."

"Nice to meet you, Mr. Salt."

"Yeah, that's what you told me before."

Black looked the man up and down from head to toe, looking back at his face. "We've met?"

"A year or so ago told you about my daughter going missing, you deemed it unimportant and turned down my case."

Black grimaced. "Although I don't recall the incident, I'm sure that couldn't have been the case."

Salt sighed. "I'm sure."

There was an uncomfortable silence. Black's phone rang, he removed it from his hip and looked at the screen. "I have to take this." Before Salt could object, he walked off.

"So, he's ignoring me again?"

"Not at all buddy, tell me about your situation."

"My situation, as you so callously put it, is that my daughter is missing, has been missing for some years now. And no one gives a damn including your partner. I call bullshit! Tell me brother why is it that you cooning for the man?"

"Wait what?"

"You heard me, Uncle Rufus."

"Calm that shit down, nothing is going to get accomplished by name-calling and yelling just start from the beginning what's your little girl's name?"

Black stepped back over to the two. "I have to bounce, meet you back at the office in a couple of hours."

Parker nodded and Black was off.

"See what I mean?" Salt said as he threw his hands in the air.

"It's nothing, this is how we work, I take the statements, relay them back to him and we take it from there, so once again you want to tell me your story or what Mr. Salt?"

***

Chapter Twenty-One

Jordan was at a sprint as he made his way down E. 63rd street towards the neighborhood cellphone shop. He rushed in and slammed the phone down on the counter. "How much for this?"

The cellphone shop owner picked up the phone and looked at it. "Is this yours?"

"I brought it in here, didn't I?"

He disregarded the answer. "Unlock it."

"I forgot the code."

"A hundred bucks."

"Bullshit, Abdul, that's an iPhone, I can get two-fifty easy."

"I have to unlock it, and refurbish it, look it has dents and scratches the screen is cracked."

"Fuck all that cosmetic bullshit, yall have a thousand new screens back there, $175."

"$135 is the best I'm going do for you cause you, my nigga."

"$140 and I won't bust ya ass, I told you about that nigga shit Abdul."

The store owner opened the cash register and removed some bills, placed them on the counter in front of Jordan. "Fuck you, I'm not Abdul, I keep telling you it's Raoul."

Jordan snatched the money from the counter. "Fuck ever, be easy my nigga, holla at you later."

Raoul shook his head, picked up the phone, and watched as Jordan exited the store.

***

Chapter Twenty-Two

Black sat on the hood of his car in front of his new office watching as the furniture delivery men moved in new furniture. It wasn't long before Parker joined him.

"What do you have to run off to take care of?" Parker asked as he scrolled through his phone reading messages.

"Went to see Pops, said this lady detective came to see him today."

"Yeah, homicide chick was at the airport?"

Black nodded. "Yeah."

"Did he say what she wants?"

"Asking about me, soft questions, said she didn't squeeze him, but you know Pops."

Parker laughed. "Yeah, the old man shut that shit down quick huh?"

Black smirked. "You already know."

"What's the deal with them man, they know damn well you ain't have nothing to do with it why are they wasting time and shit?"

"I don't know man, lazy police work, incompetent, crossing their T's and dotting their I's process of elimination…shit a combination of all three, I have no clue. What was up with Jon Salt?"

"You two have history."

Black raised an eyebrow. "How so?"

"Dude said he asked you to look into the disappearance of his little girl and you gave him the cold shoulder."

"I don't even remember him, but if he felt I snubbed him it wasn't intentional, I'm guessing since he came in his daughter was never found."

"Nope."

"What feeling did you get from him?"

Parker shrugged. "I don't know, I guess he's genuine but he's super confrontational I understand shit probably frustrating dealing with authorities but coming at people sideways is not the best way to ask someone for help."

"Until you walk in his shoes you'll never know."

Parker nodded. "I feel you, anyway I got his name, daughter's name, wife's name, the missing person's detective working his case, and his contact info said I would have you get back with him in a day or two."

"Cool, what is all this shit we are buying?" Black asked referring to the delivery men carrying in items.

"It's a business, we need sofas and chairs for the reception area, desks, chairs, computers, office phones, a couple of pictures make the place look presentable for when potential clients come in, I also took out some ads online, got a billboard ad and setup a website."

"How is all of this getting paid for?"

"The money we got from the police for the consulting fee I opened a business account and used some of that money, ran your card you gave me for some stuff, I applied for some business credit cards while you were in Nigeria, waiting on those to come in the mail."

"Let's hold off on spending any more money until we sit down and talk."

"Cool."

An alert went off on Parker's phone, he clicked the button and the video played. "What the fuck?"

"What is it?" Black asked as he jumped down from the hood of his car.

"A video, it's us...from earlier today."

Black stepped around Parker so that he could see the screen of the video as well. "That's us with Salt."

"How the hell did he film this I didn't see anyone with a camera."

"You notice he's not in it, we just hear his voice, the son of a bitch had to have had a hidden camera somewhere on his clothes."

"Is this legal?"

"Technically yes, especially if he's using it under the guise of journalism."

"That shit seems like a fringe on my privacy."

"Pendulum swings both ways, police don't like being filmed either."

"Nah bruh, that's different it's a lot of corrupt police out there."

"I'm not arguing with you just saying what's good for the goose is good for the gander, where is this posted at?"

"Looks like he has a website called Exposing Corruption, he posts videos and does blogs looks as if...yep, he posted to YouTube, and Twitter he's gone viral."

"For what?"

"You saw the video, he's claiming you're a sellout only in it for the money, if he had reward money being offered like the New Trier girls you would have made his case a priority."

"I don't need this distraction right now."

Parker continued scrolling through the website. "I don't think dude is going away easily, looking at his page he's been at it for a while he has a core following: community activists, preachers, a community of minorities parents across the country with missing children who felt wronged by the system who donate to his cause looks like he even has a few local politicians working with him."

"Those are probably photo ops if the politicians on his website in pictures."

"Either way, he probably still has their ear." Parker turned the phone towards Black. "He looks familiar to you?"

Black looked closer at the person in the photo. "No, should he?"

"Just asked, you were rubbing elbows with senators and shit just thought you might know him."

"What's his name?"

Parker turned the phone back towards himself and scrolled through the website. "Uh…Tyler Takashi-Diaz."

"Nope, doesn't ring any bells I haven't heard from my usual source since I left Nigeria would have her dig into him and Salt for me." He was referring to his long-term hacker Seshat, he helped her out with a situation when he was D.A., and she's been helping him out ever since.

"Don't worry about it let me see what I can do."

Black raised an eyebrow.

Parker smirked. "Seriously, I got this."

Before Black could object a car pulled up and parked behind his car. A man and woman emerged from the car and approached the two. The man reached out his hand to Black for a handshake.

"Mr. Love, I'm Mr. Franklin, my wife."

Black took his hand in a handshake and nodded at his wife.

"The ads are paying off already," Parker said.

Black turned to Parker. "Mr. and Mrs. Franklin this is my partner Parker, how can we help you?"

"We've never met but in the case, you were working when those girls were found, one of them was our daughter."

Black smiled. "That's great, how is your little girl?"

"Unfortunately, that's why we're here, everything was fine it was rough at first getting readjusted after everything, but we pushed through."

"Well, what's the problem?" Black asked crossing his arms across his chest.

"Shaunte didn't come home last night."

The smile faded from Black's face. "I'm assuming you called her phone and checked with her friends, right?"

"Yes sir Mr. Love, her phone just goes to voicemail and her friends haven't heard from her."

"No boyfriend."

The parents both shook their heads no. Black continued his line of questioning.

"You went to the police?"

"They said they had to wait 48 hours before anything can be done, she may come home on her own."

"Even with everything that she went through and her abductor still on the run, come on inside, so I can take down your information we'll see what we can do."

***

Tyler lay in bed naked, only a sheet covering his bottom half, he stared in awe as he watched Erica walk around the penthouse suite, they rented getting dressed.

"You are an astonishing woman."

She looked into the mirror to find his reflection staring back at her. She grimaced. Rolled her eyes. "You exaggerate so."

"Go away with me for the weekend, name a continent and I'll have my jet have us there in a few hours."

She laughed. "You're being ridiculous I have work to do and so do you."

Tyler lowered his head in defeat.

She applied lipstick to her lips and walked over to him, sitting next to him on the edge of the bed. "Don't pout."

He turned from her. She placed her hand underneath his chin and turned his head so that his face met hers, she placed a soft kiss on his lips. "Soon, let me finish my work and we shall get away to any place you like…I promise."

"I shall hold you to that."

"All I ask is that when I show you who I truly am that you don't run from me."

He laughed. "Don't be dramatic there is nothing that you could show me that would make me run from you."

"And my dear Tyler, I shall hold you to that."

***

Chapter Twenty-Three

Veronica sat across from Parker staring intently at the chess board, he held a sly smirk as the blunt stuffed with marijuana hung from his lips. "What are you going to do mama, we ain't got all night."

"Would you just hush and let me think."

He laughed. "Don't get mad at me, I told you not to move that Rook."

She contemplated for a few seconds more before making her move. "Check."

He took a pull from his blunt, held his head up, and blew the smoke toward the ceiling. "You sure you want to move there?"

"What do you mean am I sure?"

"Are you sure, it ain't a part of the rules but if you ain't sure I'll let you pull it back and move something else?"

"Boy please, just move your piece."

Parker moved his piece across the board. "Check mate." He stood from the table and walked across Veronica's living room and flopped on the couch. She sat staring at the board looking for a possible way out of the defeat. "You can look all night ain't nothing going change, that's mate."

She stayed at her spot in front of the board staring at the pieces. "Boy shut up it ain't mate nothing."

He laughed. "Come on over here and keep me company I know it won't be long before you be sitting in front of that stack of files or clicking away at the laptop. She got up from the table and joined him on the sofa, she laid her head on his lap.

She laughed. "I can't stand you."

"I hope you don't be a sore loser when you lose in court."

"You are tripping, I do not lose in court."

"Talk your shit then."

She laughed.

He offered her the blunt. "You smoking tonight?"

"You know I have a long night preparing for my case-loads tomorrow that won't do anything but make me horny and sleepy."

"That's not all bad, is it?" He asked as he gently gripped one of her breasts.

She pushed his hand away and sat up. "It is if I'm trying to get some work done." She placed a kiss on his lips. "I'm going to my office to get some work done, don't fall asleep out here on the couch."

"Don't you make me have to come in there and get you, you got until this movie goes off, we don't get that much time together."

She stood from the couch, and didn't respond. As she walked away, he smacked her across the butt. She grabbed her butt, turned around, and faced him smiling. "I heard you dang, when I hear the TV go off, I'll meet you in the room."

***

Chapter Twenty-Four

Morena sat at her desk in her home office reading notes that she had taken about patients she treated earlier that week. She was working as a therapist for the city of Chicago. Most of her cases were physically and sexually abused women and children trying to readjust to society. A saucer of torn-off crust from a sandwich and uneaten potato chips sat on her desk next to her laptop. Her television was on low tuned in to FOX 32, she wore a pair of sweatpants and an oversized Carlos Santana t-shirt.

There was a tap at the door and Teresa entered, she held two glasses of red Cabernet wine. Morena looked up, placed her pen on her desk, and welcomed Teresa into her lap, Teresa placed a kiss on her lips and handed her a glass of wine.

"How's it going in here?"

"Same as usual."

Teresa took a sip from her glass. "I don't see how you do it; I know you help people and all, but day in and day out it is so sad and depressing I would slit my wrists."

Morena laughed. "I have my days, but I push through."

Teresa sat her glass on the desk, faced Morena, and began placing kisses on her neck. "How so?" She asked in between kisses.

"I remember the good days, the days I have the breakthroughs. The days when somehow the people I've helped have slipped my mind because I've moved on to the next traumatic soul and boom someone, I've helped sends me a letter, or a photo or they pop in and tell me how well they're doing and how I saved their lives. All of that is what helps me to push through, my superpower to help make the world a better place. I get paid to listen and not judge." She laughed. "Ain't God good?"

Teresa laughed as well. "Yes, he is."

Morena took a sip from her glass. "Now that, that's out of the way, you want to tell me what's on your mind?"

Teresa pulled back from kissing Morena's neck and stood. Spoke with her back to her. "What makes you think that something is on my mind?"

"So, you're telling me that there isn't anything that you want to talk to me about?"

Teresa chuckled. She turned and faced Morena. "No, but-"

"Spit it out."

"Don't get mad but the other night when you were asleep, I went out and met Black."

Morena bit into her lip. "And?"

"And what?"

"Is there more to this confession?"

"Well, we just talked, not for very long but we spoke privately."

Morena didn't respond verbally, she nodded and finished the wine in her glass.

Teresa spoke again. "Say something."

"Something like what Teresa, you said it was private if you want me to know you will volunteer the information, I'm not going to dig."

Teresa rolled her eyes. "You aren't angry?"

"Should I be? What response did you expect, should I curse you, slap you around a little bit?"

"Of course not, I guess I expected more than this."

"Are you disappointed?"

"No, just, surprised."

"Do I have anything to worry about?'

"Of course not. I love you."

"Okay." She picked up her pen and began jotting notes again.

"Hmph…okay." She turned and faced the television. After a few moments of silence, Morena raised her head and found Teresa focused on the television. Teresa whispered. "Speak of the devil, that's Black and his friend."

"Who's filming? I recognize that voice."

Teresa shrugged her shoulders. A few seconds later the video cut to the FOX news studio, Jon Salt sat across from a newscaster answering questions.

"I trust you, as far as I'm concerned you can clear your conscience unless it's more to tell me."

Teresa shook her head no. "No." She smiled.

"I have work to finish up, I'll be into bed late."

She walked out of the room and closed the door behind her. Morena picked up her phone and dialed a number, it rang a few times and was answered. "Black, we need to talk."

***

Chapter Twenty-Five

Black was up before the sun, he rolled out of bed and dropped to the floor he heard the joints in his elbows and knees creak and pop as he began doing push-ups. It had been a while since he had worked out, he did three sets of fifty push-ups before getting up and getting in the shower. He thought about Trigger, working out made him think about her he got out of the shower, dried, and got dressed he put on black jeans and a black Naughty by Nature hoody, and a baseball cap he ordered offline he finished the outfit off with a pair of black Timberland boots. He grabbed a key lime and granola-flavored yogurt from the refrigerator and was out the door.

Now on the highway headed towards the police station to meet with detective Torres, that was the missing person's detective from the Franklins' case he called in a favor from Bunchy to help get him the meeting with the detective. It wasn't long before he was pulling into the garage, he put the car into park and kept the engine running. He got out of the car and stood in front of it, a few uniformed officers came and went, all taking notice of him but none speaking. It wasn't long before he was approached by a man short, taller than Black but not by much. His hair came down past his ears, it was uncombed and looked as if it could use a good wash. He wore tan slacks, a button-up striped shirt untucked, a tie loosely worn, blue suit jacket, covered with a tan trench coat. He carried a manilla folder and was headed straight towards Black.

"You Love?" The Hispanic officer asked Black.

Black nodded yes.

He handed Black the folder. "It's like I told the Franklins, they need to give it a couple of days she may come home, you know how young people are."

Black didn't respond, he began thumbing through the file.

Torres continued. "Well anyway, that's everything I have."

"There's not much here."

"We were looking at the boyfriend when I first got the case, he's in Cook County now."

"Thought you were going to wait 24 hours how do you know he's in the county?"

"I am a detective Love."

"Jerrika Kennedy?"

"Childhood friend, Mrs. Franklin suspected her because the two had a falling out right before Shaunte disappeared."

"She wasn't the cause of the disappearance but when you started the investigation and you spoke to her, what *"feel"* did you get from her?"

Torres placed his hands in coat pockets and removed a bag of sunflower seeds. He popped a few in his mouth and spit the shells onto the ground. He offered the bag to Black, Black shook his head no. "Genuine fear and worry for her friend, the fight was just typical high school kid shit, she loved her friend."

Black nodded. Torres nodded, walked in the opposite direction and Black got into his car, placed the file on the passenger seat, and pulled out of the garage.

Talking to the Franklins made him think about the other girls he found from the cannibal case, he felt kind of bad that he hadn't reached out to the families of the girls and seen how they were getting along since being reunited with their loved ones. His thoughts transitioned back to the list of missing girls he had stolen from the abortion clinic, the clinic where he met Stone; he had done them a dis-service as well after his trail ran cold, and he stopped looking for them. He rubbed his eyes, rolled down his window, and let the highway air hit his face. Picked up his phone and dialed Bunchy, he answered on the first ring.

"Bunch."

"Yeah, Black."

"I need another favor."

"What is it?"

"I need you to look into the girls from the cannibal case that got returned home."

"Why, you find out something about the Franklins girl?"

"Unfortunately, no, just a feeling I got, can you check for me?"

"Give me an hour." He ended the call before Black could respond.

***

Chapter Twenty-Six

Black sat in his car talking on the phone with Morena, after hanging up he dialed Stone.

"What's up, I'm downstairs come open the door."

"Hold on, I'm coming down."

Before Black could respond, the call was disconnected a few minutes later Stone was opening the passenger's side door and climbing in, she closed the door and kissed Black.

"What's up?" She asked running her hand up Black's leg.

"Shit, what's up with you?"

"Nothing, just surprised you stopped by that's all."

"I know I didn't call, but you don't want to fuck with me tonight or something?"

"It's not that but…"

"Look, if you have company already you could've said that on the phone you didn't have to come down here and-"

"Slow down nigga, it ain't like that."

"Spit it out then, tell me what it's like."

"My baby daddy is in town, he's in some trouble, it ain't like I wanted his ass all up in my shit because Lord knows I don't, but he is my kid's father."

Black shook his head solemnly. "How long is he going to be staying with you?"

"Not long."

"Umm-hmm, yall fucking?"

"Hell nah!"

"Aight man, it ain't like we made shit official or nothing like that."

"Here you go."

"I ain't tripping shorty I'm good."

She laughed. "So now I'm shorty, I don't have a name now?"

"Don't start that shit with me, you the one got niggas laid up, running up in you and shit."

"Fuck outta here with that, don't come at me like I'm just some hoe bag, it's the father of my children and we are not sleeping together."

"If you say so, I'm cool, I don't want you to keep him waiting hit me up when you get shit cleared up. ... if it gets cleared up."

"You know what, fuck you, Black, with ya jealous ass."

She opened the door, got out, and slammed the door closed. Black turned the car on, shifted into drive, and screeched off leaving Stone standing on the sidewalk seething.

***

Chapter Twenty-Seven

Jon jumped out of bed with a sunny disposition, the past few years had been hard, but things were beginning to turn around. He had a profitable blogging business he hadn't found his daughter yet, but he had managed to help assist in finding other parents' children on occasion. He stretched and made his way to the bathroom, turned the shower on, and let the water run he then made his way to the kitchen and looked out the window, the streets were serene this time of the morning, and the sun was barely up so the block was still asleep. When it awoke and people began their day-to-day routine it would be an entirely different scene. Jon grunted; Prairie Shores apartments were a far cry from his home in Ashburn but for what he had to go through to get what he wanted; it would do.

He turned the pot of coffee on and unplugged his phone from the phone charger, pressed a button and the phone rang. It was answered on the first ring.

"Hello." A man's voice answered on the other end.

"Who the hell is this?" Jon demanded.

"You know who the hell it is, and I'm not telling you again Jon, stop calling this phone!"

The call was disconnected, Jon stared at the phone, felt rage boiling in his chest, and squeezed the phone it cracked the screen. Dropped the phone and went to his shower to start his day.

"They just don't understand." He mumbled to himself as he walked down the hall. "They will though, they all will!"

***

"We have to move now!" Bunchy said to Black through the other end of the phone. "Stewart and Jones didn't even want me to call you but when we reached out to the cell phone carrier about the Franklin girl's phone and got a hit, I thought it was only right we included you in the bust."

"Thanks, man, where did it ping?"

"A cell shop on E. 63rd owned by Raoul Akhundzada, we're rolling out sirens blaring."

"I'll be there." Black ended the call, made his way out to his car, hopped in, and drove non-stop to the address that Bunchy had given him running red lights and stop signs until he reached the general area, Bunchy didn't mention the name of the store so Black just drove down 63rd until he saw a bunch of police cars. He found a place to park and rushed off towards the store along the way he dialed Bunchy and told him he was there, by the time he reached the store Bunchy was standing by the door and allowed him inside.

When Black stepped inside the store a man whom Black assumed was Raoul was handcuffed sitting next to an Afghanistan woman also cuffed. Black leaned towards Bunchy and whispered in his ear.

"Does it look like he might be the guy?"

Bunchy shook his head no. "Maybe not the main guy, but so far from the quick search of the back no physical evidence is pointing in that direction."

"How did he get the phone?"

"Says a kid sold it to him, doesn't remember his name but says it's a neighborhood kid who comes in here all the time we're going through video footage now."

"Can I question him?"

Bunchy steps away from Black and walks over to where the couple is handcuffed and whispers in Jones's ear. Jones shifts and looks back at Black, he looks back to Bunchy and nods his head up and down. Bunchy nods at Black and Black comes over.

"My name is Black Love, I'm a private detective working the case, are you Raoul?" Raoul reluctantly nods. Black continues.

"This kid that comes in, what kind of guy would you say he is?"

"I think he a good guy, is he a little wild? Yes, talk shit? Yes, but he's not like the other thugs around here he's not in a gang, he's not what you say rough type I can't see him, kidnapping girls."

An officer stepped up interrupting, he slid an open laptop across the counter they were standing in front of and pointed to the screen.

"I put in the date and time you said you think he may have come in, is that him?"

Raoul leaned in closer to the screen. "Yes, that's him."

The officer took a picture of the guy on the screen and emailed it to tech support at the police station.

"Thanks for answering my question," Black asked as he and Bunchy both stepped away back by the door.

"What now?" Black asked folding his arms across his chest.

"They're going to take her in, Jones and Stewart turning her over to ICE she has an expired work visa from 2000, he's clean here legally and has no warrants when they're done questioning and searching the premises if they buy that he has nothing to do with the guy he fingered in the video they'll cut him loose."

"You going to wait around here?"

"Yeah, at least until the questioning is done, might get a hit on who the guy is on the video, want to be in on rolling up on him too."

"How long will that take?"

"Could be anywhere from five minutes to five hours. I'm sure the FEDS are running his name nationwide but if I had to guess it shouldn't be long."

"I'm going to stick around too if that's alright, you hear anything back from the other parents of the black girls yet?"

"I did, but then this came up I put it on the backburner."

"Damn Bunch, you surprise me brother, what did you hear?"

"It's not even like that Black."

"I hear you, so what's up what did you find out?"

"Of the three girls, two are off the grid, and one is fine."

Black shook his head. "You have got to be kidding me, what happened with the other missing girl?"

"She was last seen coming out of a spoken word event over in the Loop, we knew that much because the parents found out her car was impounded when they went to pick it up, and they found out where it was towed from."

"And you think this is a coincidence?"

"Man, I don't know, it's fucking weird is what it is, if the two are connected how come body parts of black girls aren't popping up?"

"Good question-"

"We got a hit!" Jones said as he rushed past Black and Bunchy heading out the door. "Devantre Jenkins, street name Dookie last known address two blocks from here says he's on probation for a firearms charge from six months ago."

Black and Bunchy both followed the agents outside as they began piling in their cars.

"You think this Devantre is our guy?" Black asks, making his way toward where he parked his car.

"Probably not, but he has to explain to us where he got that phone," Jones says as he starts up his car and pulls off.

***

Black hit the cruise control and rode down the highway Al Green's "Simply Beautiful" blared through the speakers, he had the windows down letting the air from the highway hit his face. No destination in mind he just rode. He picked up his phone and glanced at the screen, the false leads amounted to time wasted, Parker hadn't called him all day, he picked up his phone and dialed him. He answered on the first ring.

"Where you at?"

"The office," Parker answered back. "What's up with you?"

"Thought we had a lead, found the Franklins girl's cell phone tracked it down to a cell shop, the owner pointed out a kid named Devantre Jenkins."

"How did that go?"

"About how I figured it would, no damn where, they took the kid in any way."

"Why do you think he's clean?"

"He said he found the phone when he got off the L, I believe him. Shit, he has no car, no motive, and no known connections to any of the girls that we know of especially not the white girls, I doubt it he's just hanging out in New Trier, not saying it ain't some black folks that live out there but there's a good chance that he doesn't know any of em."

"Now what?"

"I'm calling it a night, we'll re-group in the morning." Black ended the call. He thought about Stone and if he had exaggerated his response to her kid's father staying there. They weren't a couple and if he had the chance, he would spend time with Trigger if he could without giving it a second thought.

His thoughts shifted to Trigger, wondered where she was, it had been a while since they hung out. He thought about the last time he saw her, it was too brief, tried to remember the hug, she smelled good. He smiled thinking about calling her, dismissed that thought as well shifted his mind to Teresa, he was happy for her and Morena they seemed to be in a good place. He picked up his phone and dialed Morena, she answered on the first ring.

"This is Black, I'm ready to talk, meet me at my office." He ended the call and headed in that direction.

***

Chapter Twenty-Eight

Parker had spent the better half of the morning at the office arranging furniture and hanging pictures. The other half hooks up computers, printers, fax machines, and telephone lines. After getting things looking the way he wanted them to look he sat down in front of the computer and logged on to a website called humanfinder.com he typed in Jon Salt, put in his age, and let the computer do its thing, after a little under ten minutes it came back with a report.

The website was asking for a $29.95 fee, Parker input the credit card information, and the file opened. There was a list of possible relatives, addresses from the past seven years, previous employers, possibly social media pages, and arrest records.

Parker began going through the file clicking on each block reading and printing out the portions he thought might be important to Black. It said that Salt had been divorced, but he could not find anything about any children. He clicked on the social media block, and an old myspace page popped up, a Twitter page, an Instagram page, and his YouTube page associated with his blog.

Parker clicked on the Twitter page no pictures of him with a child popped up. After doing the same with his Instagram and Facebook pages and finding nothing associated with him and his missing daughter he typed in the child's name and a list of Facebook pages with women with the same name popped up. He clicked through each page, and none matched. Three were white women and one an Asian from California. He then typed in the ex-wife's name, and an Instagram page popped up he clicked on it, and it showed the woman only had three posts, one of her alone looked to be a few years old, and the other two posing with another man.

Feeling as if he was getting nowhere Parker closed all the social media pages and began clicking on the names of possible relatives just as before none appeared to match, they were all different nationalities. He got to the final name on the list Abe Booker T. Salt, said he lived in Clarksdale, MS. Parker found an address but no phone number or social media contacts, he printed out the address and logged off the computer.

***

Parker decided he would pay a trip to see the ex-wife and get her perspective on the situation. He committed her address to memory and shot Black a text telling him he would meet him in a few hours at the office. He left the items he printed out on the desk and headed out to his car, it was Pops car, he borrowed it sometime back when he was in a pinch with the law, and sort of unofficially was gifted the car he promised himself as soon as the money started flowing in regularly, he would do something nice for the old man.

Parker stood on the stairs looking out over the neighborhood, since moving in and rehabbing the old church he had gotten to know the neighbors a bit, mostly old people, kids, and women, there were not very many men around. Parker locked eyes with a face that looked familiar. A 6'11, 350 lbs., blonde-haired, Nordic-looking white guy with a crooked nose that looked like he had his share of fights on the losing end. Parker took his time moving down the stairs, he didn't know the man, but he never forgot a face it was the guy from in front of the police station. Then it clicked, he didn't just know him from in front of the police station being a dick. He was an actual dick…he was the detective that busted him and his crew and got him his case.

The detective moved from in front of his truck and met Parker halfway, they stopped a few feet from one another in the middle of the street.

"You following me officer Bosselait?"

"That's detective, felon."

Parker didn't respond, he locked eyes, with Bosselait, he was used to shakedowns, and this was no different, this was the first time since being home from prison that he wished he had a gun. The detective broke the silence.

"I'm watching you, that day I saw you outside the station what was your business with the D.A.?"

Parker raised an eyebrow. "Just that, my business."

"Don't get smart with me, you know threatening a government official is a crime punishable by-"

"Fuck all that officer, what do you want, you know damn well I didn't threaten anyone, you know my history I don't do threats, if I'm going do it, I do it."

Bosselait took a step backward, removed his gun from his holster, and placed it on the hood of his truck. He turned back to Parker. "Then do it felon-"

Before he could finish his sentence, Parker struck throwing two blows to his midsection, the blows made Bosselait take a step back as Parker moved in closer for another blow, he needed to keep the space between him and the detective small Bosselait was big but he was quicker than he looked, he struck bringing both fists down on top of Parker's shoulders, he felt his knees give before he went all the way down Bosselait picked him up off of his feet and ran across the street carrying him as Parker clawed to get free, Bosselait slammed Parker back first on the hood of his car.

Fists clenched he began raining punches down on Parker's face and chest. Parker took the blows as he fought his way back to his feet, the two men squared off, and they traded blows with Parker getting the best of him, when it came to boxing, both men bloodied neighbors began piling out of their homes a small crowd had gathered. Bosselait knew if he wanted this to end well, he would need to get his hands on him again. He rushed Parker wildly, Parker dodged the attack this time side stepping him and throwing a punch of his own he just barely missed hitting Bosselait in the ear, Bosselait stumbled losing his footing Parker rushed and punched him in the back of the head. Bosselait fell face-first landing awkwardly.

Parker now tired, but refused to show it, dropped to his knees, and wrapped his arms around Bosselait's neck from behind, locking both of his legs around one of Bosselait's legs, if Bosselait struggled to break free, Parker would break his leg. Parker squeezed his biceps around Bossealit's throat.

Parker had blacked out, the only thing he was zoned in on was him and his opponent, he no longer saw the crowd, he only saw red. He squeezed tighter.

"Parker...let him go, you're going to kill him."

He heard the faint voice, but he ignored it, and looked up at the silhouette of the small woman, her face unclear to him. She spoke again. "Let him go, fool you want to go back to prison?"

Parker loosened his grip, used one of his feet and kicked Bosselait away from him, made his way to his feet. Shook his head to clear the fog, and looked at the woman. It was Trigger, they both looked at the detective and smiled. She attempted to let him lean on her as they moved towards the office, but he pushed her away. As they reached the stairs a voice yelled out.

"Look out young man!"

It was one of the neighbors, before Parker could turn around, he was hit with a bolt of electricity, he shook and hit the ground. Trigger turned to find Bosselait standing a few feet away bloodied holding a stun gun.

***

Chapter Twenty-Nine

People often got the actions of the two detectives miscon-
strued. Jones was the loud one, aggressive, and tone-deaf so people automatically put their defenses up. Those that knew him
knew he was a gentle giant at heart. Stewart on the other hand was
a slow loris- the most innocent-looking and adorable animal ever.
But beware—this cuddly-looking creature is poisonous. They
have a small gland on the side of their elbow that will secrete poi-
son when they are disturbed, and Stewart was no different. She
used people's presumptions about her to her advantage. Although
Black hadn't wronged her in any way, there was something about
him that didn't sit right with her, he may not have done the murders or kidnapped the girls, but he knew more than he was telling
and she would find out what it was, sooner or later.

She was on her way to see his ex-fiancé Teresa Prince; she'd
found out about her when she interviewed his former colleagues
at the D.A.'s office. After a quick internet search, a small article
popped up about her rape scandal with the police in Danville, Illinois. The woman almost always gave up something, rather they
knew it or not. She didn't bother calling she didn't want her to
alert Black or worst turn her down to meet so she just popped up.

Upon reaching the home in Bronzeville, a renovated Brown-
stone, from the 20's she parked, got out of the car, approached
the door, and knocked. She leaned over the porch and peaked into
the window; she saw a short, brown-skinned woman approaching.

"Who is it?" the woman yelled through the door.

"Detective Stewart, I'm here to see Teresa Prince."

"Detective?" Teresa unlocked the door and opened it just enough to see the detective's face.

"I'm Teresa, what do you want?"

"I just have a few questions; you mind if I come in, ma'am?"

"I do, I didn't call you, what questions do you have for me?"

Stewart cleared her throat, she hadn't expected the woman to be so defensive, knowing her history with the police she should have expected as much. "My questions ma'am, are actually about Black Love, you are familiar with him, aren't you?"

"I can't tell you anything about Black, that Black can't tell you himself."

"Oh, I apologize, I thought that you were his friend…thought that you would want to help him."

Teresa inadvertently sneered at the detective. "I am his friend Detective Stewart, I'm doing what good friends do, I'm not talking to law enforcement officers about them without the advisement of an attorney. Good day." She closed the door and locked it. Stewart stared at the door seething. She looked over to the window and found Teresa staring at her, she opened her mouth to speak, but before she could mouth a word Teresa closed the curtains.

***

Chapter Thirty

Senator Tyner sat in bed wearing his pajamas with his laptop on his lap. He stared at the screen for what seemed like hours watching the blinking curser fade in and out he was contemplating sending money to his son Charles. He had no issues sending him money to stay in hiding, well crypto currency was harder to track back to him. The deal was if he left Chicago and stayed gone, he would make sure he was financially secure, he was supposed to be in a country with no U.S. extradition treaty. The senator shook his head disappointedly, he hadn't verbally spoken to his son for almost three years, and now he was back in Chicago and on this rampage with these teenage girls.

It was his flesh and blood out there causing these atrocities, he saw the funny looks they gave him at the country club and the state capital, he was an embarrassment to the Tyner name. True he wouldn't be the first Tyner to get blood on his hands but to do so publicly like a common thug was low class, he had the right mind to cooperate with the authorities and turn him in. And after all that he's done, he's now asking for ten million to leave the country again. The senator closed the laptop and placed his palms on his face. His wife had left him after the incident first occurred, went back to Iowa to be with her family, and changed her name back to her maiden name to escape the embarrassment. The senator blamed the girl, Avery it had to have been her, if only he could kill her and blame all this mess on her and clear his son's name. He wouldn't do it; he wouldn't send the money. He closed the laptop and got out of bed. Walking across his room, the door slowly crept open he found himself staring at the barrel of a 9mm Kimber micro, his eyes darted upward to the person holding the gun.

"What in the hell are you doing here?" He demanded as he moved towards the person holding the gun.

"You should've sent the money old man."

Two shots rang out both hitting their target, one in the stomach and one in the kidney.

***

Chapter Thirty-One

Parker stepped out of Division V after being held for hours, holding onto his plastic property bag as his shoes flopped, walking with no laces in them the first person he saw standing outside when he exited was Trigger. He shook his head embarrassingly.

"You hungry?" She asks as she started walking towards where she had parked.

He quickly caught up to her. "Hungry as a hostage."

"Harold's Chicken?" She asked as she pressed the button on her keychain and the doors disengaged.

"Harold's is good, thanks for bailing me out, I'll get the money back to you."

She didn't respond she opened the door and climbed inside behind the wheel.

"Parker!" A voice screamed out from behind him. He turned to find Veronica behind him walking towards him. "What's going on, what are you doing down here?" She asked as she made it to the car and looked inside at Trigger in the driver's seat. "Who is this?"

"This is Trigger, she's Black's friend and our contractor."

Trigger nodded at Veronica, Veronica rolled her eyes and turned her attention back to Parker. "So, what are you doing here?" Before he could respond she took notice of the property bag in his hand and his unlaced shoes. "Were you arrested?"

"It's a long story, I'll tell you later."

"No Parker, tell me now."

"It ain't shit babe, trust I'll tell you later, I'm tired."

She placed her hand underneath his chin and examined the bruises on his face. "We're you fighting?"

He sighed. "It's not what you think."

She took a step back. He reached out for her she pushed his hand away. "I knew it." She shook her head no. "I knew I should not have taken a chance on you."

Parker chuckled. "A chance on me?"

"A chance on this. . .you don't have anything to lose so you can get wild and be on thuggish shit, but I have a career to worry about, I am about to be General Attorney for Christ's sake I can't be wrapped up in this shit!" She said through gritted teeth.

"Girl you are tripping it's not what you think." He reached out for her again, she pushed him away.

"Don't touch me."

"You know what, I'm not in the mood for this, I'll call you later tonight."

"Don't bother!" She said as she turned and walked back in the direction that she had come from.

Parker opened the door, got in, and slammed the door closed. Trigger looked at him from the corner of her eye, turned the car on, and shifted to drive.

"Screw the chicken, take me back to the office to get my car I lost my appetite.

***

Chapter Thirty-Two

Stone wore her boy shorts, footies, and an oversized Notorious B.I.G. t-shirt, she was in the kitchen frying chicken and macaroni and cheese, and her oldest daughter Sapphire sat at the kitchen table chopping vegetables for the salad as her youngest daughter Sage stood over the sink making a pitcher of Kool-Aid. Julius her ex and the father of her kids sat on the floor, blunt between his lips playing 2K 17 with their only son Sean, Julius was supposed to have only stayed one night, it had come and gone, and he seemed as if he had no plan on leaving anytime soon.

Their other daughter, Sean's twin Si'Drew acted as the DJ, as Usher's "No Limit" went off she went into Beyonce's "Single Ladies". Stone and her three girls all immediately stopped what they were doing ran into Stone's room and returned each wearing a pair of Stone's high heel shoes, the three ladies broke off into their rendition of Beyonce's dance routine singing in unison "If you liked it then you should have put a ring on it

If you liked it then you shoulda put a ring on it

Don't be mad once you see that he want it

If you liked it then you shoulda put a ring on it

Oh, oh, oh"

Sean shook his head, and continued playing the game, he was used to the antics. His father stared wide-eyed laughing.

"Is this what you have to deal with around here son?"

"Man, they crazy they always doing stuff like that."

Stone kept dancing. She laughed. "Don't listen to them girls, they just mad they can't be a part of the Bey-hive."

"So ya'll like Destiny's Child then huh?"

"Nope, we all Beyonce!" Sage blurted as she kept dancing oversized shoes flopping and clacking against the floor with each step.

Julius laughed. "Well alright then."

They laughed and danced until the song went off, Stone kicked off her shoes and made her way back to the kitchen to take the chicken out of the skillet. Moments later the food was plated, and they all ate and talked in front of the television as they watched Ice Cube's and Kevin Hart's "Ride Along". A while after that Stone and Julius sat in her room listening to Sade. He sat on the edge of the bed as she sat in the center legs folded Indian style as they played a game of two-hand spades. They passed a blunt back and forwards to one another.

"You know I've enjoyed you guys' Stone."

She didn't respond. He continued. "It feels good being a family, know what I mean?"

Still no response, she took another pull from the joint and passed it to him, discarded a card.

"It ain't cool to you?" He asked directly once he realized that she wasn't going to respond.

"It's cool."

"Cool?"

She chuckled. "Yeah nigga, it's aight, this normal shit for us this is what families do, I mean I'm glad you're getting a kick out of it but what do you want me to say?'

He discarded a card and picked up the book. "Shit, I guess you done said it all."

She laughed. "Don't start pouting and shit nigga, fucking up my mood you can go back in the living room with the kids if you are going be on all that."

He took a pull of the blunt, stood from the bed sat the roach in the ashtray on the dresser, and came back to the bed where she sat and stood over her. She looked up with a frown on her face.

"What? Don't start acting all weird and shit."

He reached down and wrapped his hand around her neck, she placed her hands on top of his. "What are you doing?"

"You talking too much." He said as he let his body fall on top of hers and started kissing her neck, her legs parted as he positioned himself between them.

"What are you doing?" She asks in an airy breath.

"You want me to stop?"

She didn't respond verbally as she tugged at his belt.

"I missed you." He said as he pulled his shirt over his head and threw it to the floor.

"Julius."

"Yeah, babe."

"Don't talk."

He looked into her now droopy bedroom eyes, licked his lips then ripped her t-shirt open, her breasts lay there braless staring up at him.

"Negro you are buying me a new shirt."

He covered her mouth with his, ran his hands from her chest down to her belly, down further between her legs, pulled her underwear to the side, and pushed himself inside. They romped and rolled and squealed and moaned until the early morning. They laid back-to-back Julius was fast asleep. Stone lay there wide-eyed regretting her moment of weakness all she could think about was Black and how she felt like she betrayed him.

***

Chapter Thirty-Three

Jon sat down the block, in his van on W. 83rd place in Ashburn, he drew in a breath of air and then exhaled. It was a far cry from being like Glencoe, but it wasn't West Garfield Park either it was a happy medium, things still happened in Ashburn but for the most part, it was a community of hard-working, church-going black folks. A place to raise a family, his family which was stolen from him, first his little girl then his wife. They would pay, they would all pay in due time he thought to himself as he watched his ex-wife exit the home they once shared followed by her new man. They got into separate vehicles and pulled off, Jon started his van and followed behind the man's car.

***

Chapter Thirty-Four

When Black pulled up, he saw the taillights of Parker's car, turning the corner at the end of the block. He was about to call his phone but dismissed the thought when he looked in his rear-view mirror and saw that Morena was pulling up behind him to park. He got out of the car and headed up the stairs and unlocked the door. A few moments later Morena was beside him as he held the door open for her to enter.

"This is a nice space Black; this looks good, I am impressed."

"Thank you, I didn't have a hand in it, it was Parker."

He led the way past the waiting area up the flight of stairs to the office he had picked out for himself. The room was large but simple, with a black leather sofa and loveseat, a coffee table, and a desk with a laptop, printer, and landline phone. A stack of papers sat in the center of the desk. Black picked them up and joined Morena on the sofa.

"So, what do you want to talk about?" Black asked as he thumbed through the papers that Parker had left for him.

"It's about the news piece I saw last night about you."

"What about it?"

"I know the guy who filmed you."

"Jon Salt?"

"Yeah."

"How so?"

"He and his wife came to see me a few years back they were having issues with their marriage."

"He ever mentions anything about their missing daughter?"

"Her daughter."

"Excuse me?"

"Her daughter, it was his step-daughter, and yes that's why they were there the disappearance of Kia was taking a toll on the two. Well anyway, I can't ethically comment on the specifics of their sessions, but I can say that the two are not together anymore and as far as Kia goes the mother has moved on, he has not."

"What made you want to tell me this?"

"A gut feeling about Jon, he never expressed it straightforwardly but reading between the lines he struck me as very vengeful."

"You think he may be connected to these girls?"

She shrugged her shoulders. "I don't know, just telling you that we crossed paths and passing on the little bit of information that I can give you."

"Well according to the medical examiner's report apart from the victims that had messages carved into them, the ones that had the limbs severed had to be done by someone with medical experience. Do you know what he did for a living before becoming an internet activist?"

"He was no doctor I can tell you that, if I remember correctly, he worked as a janitor at some elementary school, can't remember the name of it."

"Janitor huh?"

"I'm pretty sure of it, guess that rules him out."

"Unless he has an accomplice, it never sat right with me that these attacks on these girls are so vastly different as if two attackers were acting in tandem."

Black continued looking through the papers that Parker left for him. "Is that all you can tell me?"

"Yes, just wanted to put it on your brain about Jon and his compulsiveness with Kia's disappearance."

"You sure that's all you wanted to tell me?"

She stood to her feet. "Why would you think that there is anything more?"

"Because you asked to meet, you could have told me about these things over the phone or in a text. So, tell me, what's up?"

She smiled sheepishly. "Nothing more just wanted to see you in person, without Teresa."

"Why, what did you have in mind?"

She laughed. "Nothing, just that after seeing you and having dinner it made me realize how much I missed the alone time we used to have, I don't know I guess I was just being silly."

Black smiled. He didn't respond verbally. After several seconds of awkward silence, Morena continued.

"Well, let me go, Teresa will be wondering where I am."

Black wrapped his arms around her and kissed her on the cheek. "Thank you for the information I'll see if it helps any and thanks for coming to see me, I appreciate it. Tell Teresa I said hi and you are welcome anytime with or without Teresa, you hear me?"

She pulled back from the hug. "I hear you, talk soon, and maybe we'll have another dinner party, I'll host next time."

"Sounds like a plan."

He walked her back out to her car and watched as she pulled off.

***

Chapter Thirty-Five

Stewart sat in her car, marveling at the homes in the Gold Coast Community of Chicago, she thought to herself my salary could not get me a closet in the pool house in a neighborhood like this. She climbed from her vehicle, closed the door, and made her way to the address she was looking for. Senator Tyner, the father of Charles Tyner primary suspect in the teenage missing girls' case a few years back. Black had worked the case and had some interactions with the son, he may have had contact with Charles, but she knew him being a Senator she would have to tread lightly. She rang the doorbell, and looking at the handle of the door, she noticed smudged blood. She drew her weapon and nudged the door open.

"Police!" She yelled out as she moved through the home, she removed a radio from her hip and pressed a button, spoke into it.

"This is detective Stewart, 38 E. Elm St. possible B & E requesting backup."

"Copy, back-up is on the way." The dispatcher replied through the radio. She placed the radio back onto her hip and continued searching the home room, by room on the first floor. After finding no one, she made her way back to the front of the home where she had seen a set of spiral stairs, she climbed the stairs and began going from room to room, until she reached the end of the hall, where there was a door open, she stepped in to find a man lying in a pool of his blood, blood blanketed his face, neck, and chest, she looked down and saw blood seeping from his lower thighs, at least it looked that way, she couldn't see where it was coming from. She lowered her weapon.

"Is there anyone else here, who did this to you?" Stewart yelled as she moved cautiously towards him.

He tried to speak but began to choke, gurgling on his blood.

"Don't talk, remain calm I'm calling for help." She holstered her weapon and removed her radio she called dispatch to send an ambulance.

***

Chapter Thirty-Six

Veronica sat on her Ottoman alone, a glass of Merlot in hand, Keyshia Cole played in the background, the television tuned to CNN, on mute. She stared at the screen thinking about her future and if it was enough room for her political ambitions and Parker and everything that came with him.

She had been District Attorney long enough to know that with every situation that there were always gray areas and she wondered if she had reacted without giving him a chance to explain his part in what went on. She chuckled to herself, she didn't know what was going on, and she never gave him a chance to explain. She could pull his arrest record it would be easy enough or she could swallow her pride, apologize, and allow him to tell her himself.

She took a swallow from her glass and set the glass on the table. She was taken out of her thought by a knock at the door, it startled her she was so lost in thought she didn't know how long that they had been knocking. She laid her head back against the ottoman closing her eyes. She didn't feel like being bothered when she realized it could be Parker coming to work things out.

Her eyes sprang open, and she leaped to her feet, rushing to the door she snatched it open, her mouth open in surprise feeling deflated she slouched her shoulders. Staring back at her was her ex.

"What are you doing here Richard?" She asked as she turned and headed back to her spot on the ottoman.

He came in behind her closing the door and following her into the living room.

"It's good to see you too."

She picked up the bottle of Merlot and poured another glass. "I'm not in the mood, what can I do for you?"

"Damn, why so cold Ronnie?" That's what he called her.

"A lot on my mind."

He chuckled. "Yeah, I bet."

She raised an eyebrow. "What does that mean?"

"You could do better is all I'm saying."

She stood to her feet. "Stop fucking around Richie and tell me what you're getting at."

"Let's just say, that the con you've been running around with won't be bothering you anytime soon, you may be hurt now, but you'll thank me later."

"You son of a bitch, it was you!"

"Listen, Ronnie, I-"

"It's Veronica."

"Veronica, I just went over there to have a few words with your "friend" and next thing I know he's taking a swing at me, a big mistake on his part had to show him how we do things in Major Crimes."

She laughed as well. Placed a hand underneath his chin. "The way your face looks, it looks like he showed you a thing or two about how things are done on the South Side."

He pulled back from her touch angrily. "I've had worst."

"I'm sure, and this proves what?"

"That I still love you and have your best interests at heart, I'm not giving you up without a fight Ronnie."

She smirked. "So, you two grown-ass men out fighting in the middle of the street like high school boys?"

"It's like I said Ronnie-" She cut her eyes at him. He continued. "I'm sorry, Veronica, like I said I came to talk, he swung at me first."

"I'm extremely disappointed in you Richard, I made it clear that we are done, and I don't appreciate you harassing and attacking my friends. If you come anywhere near me or Parker again, I will see to it that I have your badge and if I must pull every string, I have in my arsenal I will see to it that no other department in the country hires you, you'll be doing security at Dollar Tree."

He placed his meaty finger in her face. "Now wait a minute."

She slapped his hand away. "No, you wait, I thought we could be cordial, but you won't let go."

"I was giving you time to get your head together, but you don't know what's best for you."

"Best for me? Get my head together, man you sound like a fool."

"First it was that Black Love guy, at least he was a lawyer."

"Fool, are you following me?"

"It's not what you think."

"Not what I think? Richard, just go okay."

"Veronica let's talk."

"I just want you out of here."

He glowered at her for several seconds, and when he saw that she was matching his gaze he lowered his head and moved towards the door. She followed behind grabbing the door once he was on the other side of the door. He turned and faced her.

"I am sorry; I didn't know what to do to get you back."

Floyd Sr.

"There is no getting me back if you want to make it right with me and you, make it right with Parker he has enough going on in his life with trying to readjust after doing time he doesn't deserve drama on his plate that he didn't go looking for."

"Whatever you want Ronnie."

She rolled her eyes and closed the door.

***

Chapter Thirty-Seven

Stone sat on the toilet staring blankly at the wall, Julius was on the other side of the door banging.

"Let me get in girl, you've been in there almost thirty minutes now, that's a mean dookie you are taking." He said then laughed.

She rolled her eyes, he could be so crude sometimes, she thought as she looked down at the pregnancy test angrily.

"Come on, stop fucking around." He said again with another tap at the door.

"Give me a minute." She said as she stood to her feet, wrapped the test in toilet paper, and placed it into the trash can underneath the rest of the trash. She washed her hands and flushed the toilet. When she opened the door, he was standing on the other end goofy smile plastered on his face, he leaned in to kiss her, but she stiff-armed him avoiding his kiss. "Not right now, I'm not in the mood."

"Who put you in the bad mood? Aunt flow must be visiting." He remarked referring to her monthly menstruation.

She shook her head and kept walking. "What we not going do is discuss the functions of my body like it's a freaking free for all."

"Here you go." He said as he went into the bathroom and closed the door. He looked at himself in the mirror. Then slowly let his eyes scan the bathroom. He let the lid down on the toilet and sat down. He stared at the wall, something didn't seem right, Stone was acting weird.

Floyd Sr.

He stood, raised the lid, used the bathroom, and flushed. He was headed back out into the living room when he paused. Turned to the trashcan and dug through it, finding the pregnancy test.

"I can't believe this shit."

***

Chapter Thirty-Eight

Jon had been following his ex-wife's new boyfriend for days now, he smiled to himself thinking about what he was going to do to him, he would get it a lot worse than the girls he took. It would be so easy, to catch him coming out of the gym on Pulaski, a syringe of carfentanil tranquilizer, toss him in his trunk, and off to his warehouse in Gary. Or cut the brake line to his car, and let the brake fluid slowly leak until his brakes were inoperable preferably on the freeway, that was too risky his ex-wife rode in that car at times.

He could pop up in the backseat while he was driving, a plastic bag over the head. Gun him down in the streets, and drop a gun, and drugs on the dead body the police wouldn't look any further and label it gang-related or a drug transaction went wrong.

Jon laughed thinking about the endless possibilities., everything would go his way: the police would be forced to look for his little girl, the boyfriend would be out of the way permanently, his wife would realize how much she missed him, and they would get back together. He stared at the gym waiting, opened the glove compartment box stared at the pair of leather gloves and syringe filled with carfentanil.

"Not personal enough." He said to himself, he closed the glove compartment put the car in drive, and pulled off.

***

Chapter Thirty-Nine

Black didn't know what to make of the information that Morena had given him, that with the things that Parker left for him on Salt and looking into the Franklins' missing daughter, the missing girls, the victims with different assault wounds nothing was adding up. He needed to regroup, he dialed Parker it was answered on the first ring.

"What's up?" Parker said through the phone.

"I'm at the office, swing by we need to put our heads together and see if we can make sense of any of this stuff with the New Trier girls."

"Cool, I'm just driving around thinking anyway, I'm on my way."

Black ended the call and made his way downstairs to the kitchen looked in the refrigerator, it seemed as though Parker had thought of everything, the fridge was stocked with lunchmeat and cheese, Lunchable, juice, bottled water, fruit, and yogurt. He grabbed a turkey Lunchable, a Capri Sun juice pouch, and two oranges made his way to the waiting room, and sat eating waiting for Parker to arrive. In between eating, he went over the papers Parker left once more. The sound of windchimes came through a text message alert. He looked at the phone it was from Stone, he ignored it and set the phone back down.

***

Chapter Forty

Chirps from sirens, then cherries from the police lights lit up the back of Parker's car.

"Here we go again," Parker said as he pulled to the side of the road and placed the car in park, keeping his hands on the wheel at 10 and 2. Flanked on both sides of his vehicle were detectives Stewart and Jones. On the passenger's side, Jones shined a flashlight into the window with his other hand on his gun. Stewart stood on the driver's side. She tapped the window. Parker shook his head annoyed. He rolled down the window.

"Officers."

"That's detectives, where are you going?"

"Why did you stop me?"

"You have this thing reversed; we ask the questions you answer," Jones said as he shined the flashlight into the backseat of his car.

"Don't worry about it partner, we'll get him violated, I'm sure his homies at Joliet are there waiting on him," Stewart said, placing her hand on her gun. Parker remained silent; he gripped the steering wheel tighter. Stewart continued. "There, now he seems a bit more cooperative.

"Always, what can I do for you detectives?" Parker said through clenched teeth.

"I know the powers that be wanted Love on this New Trier girls' case, and if we get Love, we get you by default."

"And?"

"It doesn't sit right with me."

Parker fumed but remained silent. Stewart continued. "Let's face it, you're a mid-level gangster has been, we don't want you, give us Black, help us find the other girls and we'll see to it that the D.A. knows you did us a solid."

"Oh yeah, you'll do that for me?" Parker reached up and pulled down his sun visor, both detectives drew their weapons and had them aimed at Parker. He held a business card between two fingers with his other hand in the air. "Got damn, you two need to relax."

Stewart hesitantly lowered her weapon and holstered it. Jones kept his aimed at Parker's face. Parker handed the card out the window to Stewart. She took the card and read it.

"District Attorney Veronica Malone."

"Yeah, she's my legal representation, you can direct any questions you have for me to her. I mean unless I am under arrest right now."

Jones lowered his weapon. Stewart nodded at Jones, turned, and headed back to her car.

"Slow this piece of shit down next time alright," Jones said as he holstered his weapon and joined his partner.

"Fuck you," Parker said as he rolled his window up, placed the car into drive, and pulled off.

***

Twenty minutes later Parker was back at the office, he walked in to find Black going over the files he left, they nodded at one another. Parker sat in a chair across from Black.

"What happened to your face?" Black asked referring to the scars from the fight.

"It ain't nothing, I don't want to talk about it now. What's the plan?" Parker asked as he scrolled through his phone.

Black didn't press, he respected Parker's boundaries, and when he wanted to let him in on it, he would. "I read the stuff you left for me."

"Wasn't much there."

"I know, Morena stopped by to see me."

"You're hooking up with your ex?"

Black shook his head no. "Nah, she said she knows Jon Salt."

"Straight up, what she say?"

"Not much, she saw him and his ex in couple's therapy and couldn't tell me much you know the doctor-patient confidentiality laws."

"What did she tell you?"

"She got the vibe from him that he was vengeful, and the missing girl he's looking for wasn't his biological daughter, he seems to be the only one holding on to the thought of finding her according to Morena the ex-wife has moved on."

"And this information helps us how?"

"Not sure if it does, just laying what we got on the table."

"What about the Franklins, what did the detective have to say?"

"About as helpful as Morena was with what she had to say."

"So, a bunch of pieces to puzzles that all seem to go to different puzzles."

"Pretty much."

"Where do we go from here?"

"It's funny you say that what do you say about going to Clarksdale, MS?"

"I say I'm still on paper."

Black laughed. "You scared?"

"Nah, but why risk it, why can't you go?"

"I need to follow up on the Franklin lead, then start from scratch with all the evidence from the very first kidnapping of the New Trier girls up to now, we're done with that interviewing shit. I mean I can go; you want to stay here and work with the police?"

Parker laughed. "Nah, I've met my quota of dealing with police for the month."

Black raised an eyebrow. "Cool, in and out holler at Jon's grandfather, keep your head low, and get on back it should be smooth."

Parker pulled up the GPS on his phone. "Says it is an eight-hour drive, I can get there and back in a day."

Windchimes again. Black looked at his phone another text from Stone. He ignored it once more, a knock at the door.

"You expect anyone?" Parker asked as he watched Black move towards the door.

"Nope, you?"

Parker didn't respond, he scrolled through his phone text messages. Black got to the door and yelled. "Who is it?"

"Detective Bosselait"

"Not this guy again," Parker said as he stood to his feet readying himself for a round two bout.

"What are you talking about?" Black said as he opened the door." As soon as he saw Bosselait's face he put two and two together. "What do you want detective?"

"Can I come in?"

Black stepped to the side and allowed him entry. He spoke again. "What do you want detective?"

"I came to make things right."

Parker stepped to Bosselait. "Yeah."

"Yeah. Look, I should have been the bigger man and let you have her, I was out of line coming here and confronting you."

Black remained silent, he knew the two had history he thought the confrontation might have been old beef from Parker's arrest he had forgotten that Bosselait and Veronica were once a thing.

"What you want to hug it out now or some shit?" Parker asked eyes fixated on Bosselait.

"Let's not go that far, but a handshake is good." He offered out his hand.

Parker stared at it for several seconds before reaching out and accepting it. Both men clutched one another's hands tightly. Bosselait tried to manhandle Parker trying his best to yank Parker forward, but he didn't budge. "Let me tell you this, it took a lot for me to come here and eat crow, but Ronnie is important to me and if you hurt her in any way, it won't be back to a cell for you, I'll put you where you won't be found."

"Let me tell you, officer, if we ever lock horns again I will lay you down again, but next time it'll be for the final count."

Neither said a word, they let go of the handshake and stared one another down.

"Well, you said what you had to say Bosselait, you can go," Black said folding his arms across his chest.

Bosselait made his way back to the door and turned to face the men before leaving. "I don't see how you two do it?"

"Do what?" Black asked.

"My Ronnie is a hell of a woman; I don't see how Parker doesn't get jealous knowing that you were sleeping with her first." He shrugged his shoulders. "I guess the saying is true huh, bros over hoes, night fellas." He turned and left; Black closed the door behind him. He turned back to face Parker. Black didn't say anything, they just stared at one another. Parker tilted his head to the side.

"You're not even going to deny it."

"I wanted to tell you man when you brought her to my place that night that's what we were talking about by the door, she asked me not to tell you."

"Fuck her and what she wanted, we been boys since grade school, fought back-to-back against chumps in the street, how can you keep something like this from me?"

Black stood lips clenched looking for the right words. Parker broke the silence.

"You know what man, it doesn't even matter, yo I'm out."

He attempted to pass Black, but Black stood in his way blocking the door. Parker's hands clenched into fists.

"We are not about to do this man, the best thing to do is get out of my way before we end up doing some shit either of us can take back."

Black sighed. Stepped to the side. Parker opened the door and walked out.

***

Chapter Forty-One

Jones made his way through the base of operations at the Broadway Armory Park to his partner Stewart sitting at her makeshift desk typing out a report on her laptop.

"What's going on with you Stewart, I thought we were partners."

She didn't look up she continued typing. "We are."

"We are, are we?"

She glanced at him and then went back to typing. "Is there something you're working your way up to asking me?"

He reached over and closed her laptop. She smirked, swiveled in her chair, and faced him folding her hands and placing them on her chest. He pulled up a chair and sat facing her.

"Why do I have to hear from everyone but my partner about her bringing in a shot-up Senator who happens to be the father of a person of interest in one of the biggest abduction/murder rings in the city?"

She laughed. "You're making this bigger than what it is."

"Don't do that."

She shrugged her shoulders. "Do what?"

He pointed a finger in her face. "That shit right there, don't fucking do it, we're partners Stewart no more of this cowboy loner shit."

She rolled her eyes. "Aright, alright I got you."

"I'm serious Stewart."

"I said I fucking got you, Jones Jesus Christ have you had enough of chewing my ass out or what?"

Jones stared for several seconds before responding.

"You want to fill me in on what's going on in the streets being that I've been like your bitch around here doing inhouse shit you know interviewing and siphoning through bullshit leads…you know the fun part of police work."

She laughed. "Fun like hemorrhoids, really nothing to tell went to see one of Black's exes, that was a dead end."

"You still shaking that tree?"

"That tree, as you put it, placed me on the senator's door there's no way that shooting is not connected."

"The senator say anything?"

She laughed. "He tried."

"I don't get it, what's the joke?"

"The perpetrator cut out his tongue."

"And you laugh, that's kind of harsh ain't it?"

"Fuck him, I'm going to get a judge to sign off on a warrant to check his bank statements there's no way you can pay me to believe he isn't somehow getting money to that son of his."

"Good luck with that, there's no world you live in that a judge is going to sign off on a warrant against a U.S. senator unless you have the proverbial smoking gun, or someone owes you a favor you find anything at the senator's house you can use to get the warrant?"

She shook her head no.

"What about favors, anyone owes you any favors who has pull with a judge or at the state house?"

"Does, one of my snitches off of State Street count?"

Jones laughed. "I doubt it."

"Then I guess we're going to have to go off of prayer or luck."

"Assuming we don't get the warrant and the senator doesn't bite the bullet, where do we go from here? You want to keep chasing down the Love angle?"

"I can't shake it something is not right with that guy, I have one more person to question, don't know what it is but he's dirty."

***

Chapter Forty-Two

Erica pulled into the garage of the abandoned factory that she purchased before moving back to the states from Canada it was a steal, if Gary, Indiana wasn't such an eyesore on the map she would consider moving there, it was a good thing it was just a skip over the border to Chicago.

As she pulled in and powered off her vehicle, she was met by Jon Salt. She climbed from the car wearing a satin red dress and matching pumps a gold bracelet dangled from her wrist.

"Well, ain't you fancy, off to the ball Erica?"

She rolled her eyes and faked a smile. "I am, the policemen's ball."

He took a step back. "You're kidding right?"

"Do I ever kid?"

"Don't you think that's a little reckless, why put your head inside the lion's mouth?"

"Jon if you haven't learned by now, I am the lion."

"Listen I appreciate you funding everything and supplying me with this place, but I don't think the cops are going to come around to seeing things my way, I mean when has a Black man ever gotten justice from the white establishment?"

"Listen, Jon, I know you didn't call me here to sing me the poor black man blues. You want something you have to take it, by force if necessary."

"I get all that, that's easy to say for some rich white woman, you have everything, to be honest, I for the life of me can't figure out what you get out of this anyway."

"That's my business, I told you I can help shed light on your daughter's disappearance, didn't I?"

"You did, but I've done all of this, and nothing has come of it."

"Patience, Jon, just a little longer, the light will be shed in the end."

***

Chapter Forty-Three

Veronica was laid out on her living room sofa, Waiting to Exhale playing on the television, half-drunken bottle of wine on the floor near the sofa. She sat up when she heard a knock at the door. She reached down and picked up her phone from the floor near the bottle of wine. She looked at the time.

"1 a.m., who is coming over this late without calling? I swear if this is Richard again, I hope he is prepared to get his feelings hurt."

She mumbled to herself angrily as she made her way to the door, looked through the peephole, and opened the door. They stared at one another for a beat. "We just going look at each other or can I come in?"

She turned and walked back into the living room leaving the door open for him to enter. He followed behind closing the door behind him. She flopped down on the couch, and he sat next to her, neither looking at the other nor saying a word. Several seconds passed before Veronica broke the silence. "I overreacted."

"Why?"

She rubbed her palms together. "I don't know."

He shook his head. "Nah, keep it real with me you blew up on me for a reason."

She turned and faced him. "I'm sorry Parker, I don't know why I behaved the way I did, I saw you getting into the car with that woman. Then saw the bruises on your hands and face. You told me you had just gotten out of jail; it was all a bit much."

"Once again you're not keeping it real with me, you're a lawyer you're used to high-stress situations I'm not buying this was about me with some woman, you don't strike me as the jealous type."

She smiled awkwardly. "I'm not." She reached over and touched his face where his bruises were. He pushed her hand away.

"Don't."

"Did I hurt you?"

"Nah, I feel like you're trying to deflect keep talking."

She folded her legs Indian style, on the couch then folded her arms across her chest. "What do you want to talk about? I'm trying to apologize."

He laughed. "That's what you're trying to do?"

"Are you trying to pick a fight with me?"

"I'm trying to give you the chance to woman up and keep it real with me about everything."

"Keep it real with you, I haven't been?"

"Is that a question or a statement?"

She rolled her eyes. "Here you go, if you have something you want to say spit that shit out."

"Alright you got a pussy-whipped ex, I get that I mean we all got a past."

She shook her head up and down in agreement. "And…"

"And why I got to find out from your pussy whipped ex, about you and Black messing around?"

Veronica's mouth opened in shock. "Parker I-"

He cut her off. "You what? Was never going to tell me."

"I had no intentions of telling you because there's nothing to tell, it was a one-and-done thing."

"You should have told me, have me around here looking stupid."

"I had no intention to make you look or feel stupid."

"Veronica, that's exactly what you did so I don't give a fuck about what your intentions were."

She lowered her head. He continued. "So, you and the white boy."

"What about him?"

"You love him?"

"No."

"No? The way he was fighting over you it was like you stole a piece of his heart."

"Richard and I were a thing; a different type of thing I can't explain it I've told him things that I would probably never tell you...we shared a different type of intimacy."

"Hmm."

She smiles. "I've done things to you I'd never do to him...passionate wise."

"He never hit?"

"Never even smelled it."

"Hmm…"

"What?"

"Is that a win for me or a win for him?"

"A win-lose for you both."

He laughed. "How does a person get a win-win with you?"

She placed her hand underneath his chin until their eyes met. "Become the man I want to give both to."

***

Chapter Forty-Four

Black was headed to the station to finally follow up on the lead with the Franklins and try to piece together the rest of the evidence. He opened the door to his place to step out and found himself face to face with Stone.

"You don't know how to return messages?"

"I don't have time for this shit right now."

"You're going to talk to me now, or not at all, I'm not going to chase you, Black."

Black took a step back into his place and she followed closing the door behind her. He sat on the sofa she sat next to him and ran her hand up his thigh.

"I'm sorry, is that what you want to hear, I was wrong?"

"I don't want to hear none of it for real, it is what it is."

She chuckled. "Here you go, Mr. tough-ass Black Love, don't care about nothing or nobody."

She kept caressing his thigh, he felt an erection growing in his pants. He pushed her hand away. "You said that I didn't."

"If that's not how you feel, tell me what it is then."

"You have other situations going on, I refuse to be a part of you having kids is one thing, but I don't do the baby daddy in and out the picture shit, I don't need that in my life."

She laughed caressed his thigh again grabbed a handful of his manhood. "You are such a drama queen, there is no in-and-out situation going on, he's gone."

He pushed her hand away and stood. "I'm not playing games with you Stone."

"Games? We've been messing around for a while now; you've never claimed me and let it be known this is where you want to be full-time. And as far as my kids go, yeah you know who they are, but we've rarely spent time together all of us and I've never asked you for a dime to help provide for them nor have you offered. Keep it real Black I'm single and I can do what I want to do."

He threw his hands in the air. "Why are you here Stone?"

She stood, facing him. Pushed him to the sofa. Dropped to her knees, unfastened his pants, zipped them down, and pulled his member from his jeans. She stood, raised her skirt, and sat on top of him.

"I missed you. This is where I wanted to be, here with you, and nothing is going on with my ex I promise you. He had drama in the streets and needed a place to stay until the heat cooled down and now, he's gone."

Most of what she said was true, and knowing that made her feel a little better but what she had to do next didn't sit 100% right with her, but he was gone, and she had to make the right moves for her and her family. She wasn't sure that she was going to do this until she came home from work and saw that he was gone and found the pregnancy test sitting on the bathroom sink, right at that moment it was almost as if Julius, her ex had decided for her.

***

Chapter Forty-Five

After the meeting with Erica, Jon was growing more and more impatient with her plan, he didn't see a clear end game and that didn't sit right with him. Other than the fact that she was keeping her motives behind helping him a secret, there was something else she was holding back he couldn't explain, but he knew it was something, he convinced himself that whatever it was whenever it was revealed that it would be worth it if it helped get his little girl back. He told himself if she had her secret plans it didn't matter because he had his secret plans to get his family back. He laughed inwardly as he sat in the dark silently watching the figure fumble around the basement looking for the circuit breaker, with only the light from his phone to guide him. By the time he noticed Jon it was too late, Jon struck him repeatedly with a knife to his stomach and midsection, he kept jabbing until the man went limp and he had no more fight left.

***

Chapter Forty-Six

Parker looked at his phone, he saw Black's name flash across the screen as it rang, he let it go to voicemail and tossed it on the passenger seat. He continued driving down, US-61 S/S 3rd St entering Mississippi, after the conversation with Veronica the night before he drove all night to get to Clarksdale to meet with Salt's grandfather. He could have called but he knew that confronting a person face to face had a different effect when trying to get information out of the person versus speaking on the phone. Pulling into the town, Parker slowed his pace taking it all in, he had done some research on the town before going there, and he learned that it was a population of about 17,000 people, almost 80% of the population is Black Clarksdale was kind of a town stuck in time most of the factory jobs had fled to other cities the two biggest being Cooper Tires and Rubber, so poverty was a big factor in the small town.

He somehow ended up in downtown Clarksdale, he drove past a treasure trove of Blues bars and music stores, and he rolled past the Rock and Blues Museum. He looked at his watch, he didn't have much time he needed to find the old man and get back to Chicago the longer he stayed the more likely he had of being caught out of state without permission on parole. After driving another twenty minutes the GPS had him pulling up to a plantation-style home, that looked like it had seen better days.

There was a Cadillac of that year shining in the sun, looked as if it had just come off the showroom floor. Parked in front of it was a hearse. Parker parked behind the Cadillac and got out. He made his way onto the porch and opened the screen door he raised his fist to knock on the door, and when he heard the door unlock, he took a step back as the door slowly opened. He threw his hands in the air as he found himself staring down the barrel of a Vietnam-era M1911. 45 caliber automatic pistol.

"Hold on, old man be careful with that thing."

"Don't you worry about me being careful, I ain't never killed a man I ain't want to kill, ask them Vietcong. What are you doing out here?"

"My name is Parker; I drove out from Chicago I need to ask you a few questions about your grandson Jon."

The old man kept the gun trained on Parker. "Jon, he ain't got no friends named Parker."

"Sir, if you just put the gun down, we can talk."

"How about we don't, you just go on and get back in this piece of a shit car of yours and make that drive back to Chicago."

"I can't do that sir, it has to do with his missing step-daughter, I just want to help."

He lowered his weapon and allowed him to come in, walking behind the old man through the dimly lit home, Parker took it all in the home was massive, and a lot of old woodwork made up the ceiling beams. He had pictures and paintings that looked as if they came from a time even before the old man's time. All looked like they could have been past relatives, all black. There was one old painting of an old white man in a Southern Civil War rebel uniform. Parker raised an eyebrow, he wanted to ask the reason behind that photo and who it was but kept it to himself.

The home smelled like fresh fried bacon and biscuits.

"I was just about to eat, you hungry boy?"

"I'm fine sir, I don't want to take too much of your time I 'm on a bit of a time restraint."

The old man stopped, turned, and faced Parker. "Which one is it, you don't want to take too much of my time, or is you on a time restraint?"

Parker smiled. The old man was sharp. He looked to be 75 years old or so, face and head covered in gray hair. "On second thought I'd love to join you for breakfast, sir, what are we having?"

"Bacon and biscuits, ain't got no eggs or grits."

"It smells good, truth is I haven't eaten since leaving Chicago and drove all the way here only stopping for gas."

"Well, there's plenty here, now you ain't one of them prissy up North tofu vegetarians, are you?"

Parker laughed. "No sir, I eat meat just fine."

"Well good, I have some good old-fashioned thick-cut bacon and homemade biscuits and syrup."

"Sounds good to me sir."

Wasn't long before the two men were sitting at a round wooden table in the dining room with plates of five biscuits a piece and piles of bacon sitting in front of them. Both men drank coffee as they talked.

"What you want to know young man?"

"My detective agency is working independently of the Chicago police department and we're taking a different route regarding the investigation. We read the report the police have on file, but we'd like to know more intimate details."

He licked the syrup from his fingers before responding. "Intimate in what way?"

"How did Jon and his stepdaughter get along?"

"I can't answer that I only met the child once, they seemed to get along alright."

"Only once, you and Jon not getting along?"

"We got along alright, as well as we could I suppose being that he's ashamed of me and where he comes from."

"He told you that?"

"Not in words, but a man knows. Anyway, he ain't been back here in some time. You would think that he would be more appreciative we the only kin either of us got."

"What happened to his folks?"

"His pa was killed overseas fighting the Taliban's, his ma they took her long ago mind never was quite right after that, looney bin never did let her loose last I hear she still in there."

Parker took a swig from his cup. "You never visit?"

"Don't make much sense, her mind is in and out and I'm an old man with not much going on in my life, so I figured if I go what is there to talk about? I don't like awkward situations."

"Jon never calls?"

"Maybe once every six months or so, you would think he would take more of an interest being that all of this going be his when I'm gone."

Parker grimaced and looked around the place. Smiled.

"Don't look like that boy, it might not look like much, but this is a prosperous business."

"Excuse me."

He shook his head apathetically. "You see that hearse out front?"

"I did."

"This here is a funeral home; we've been burying folks for over four generations. I'm too old to do any of the work nowadays I got a staff and another building where they prep the bodies and hold the services. Was a time when we did everything right here in this house. Hell, I taught Jon the ins and outs of the business."

"Really?"

"Yeah, he knows everything I know."

"No shit, he knows his way around a body, how to cut em up and all that formaldehyde the whole nine yards? Did he go to school for that?"

He laughed. "Don't need schooling around these parts, folks not too particular out here long as you respectful to their deceased loved one's folks don't ask. At least not back then anyway and not when I was teaching Jon my new folks went to school for that and such."

Parker stood, and reached out his hand for a handshake. "Thank you for the meal, and the wonderful hospitality."

He stood as well and took Parker's hand into his in a firm handshake. "That all?"

"Yes sir, have a nice little ride to get back to Chicago I should get going."

"Be careful son, good luck finding that child, and tell that grandson of mine to call me more often."

"Will do sir."

Parker exited the way he entered and pulled back off the property back onto the road that brought him there heading back towards the highway to take him home.

***

Chapter Forty-Seven

Veronica was having second thoughts about not stepping down as D.A. as she ran her campaign, she was thinking more about the optics than about the amount of work that she would have to put in if it was a man in her position running for office and being district attorney at the same time he could step down as the D.A. no big deal. But her being a woman she had to make the impossible look effortless she tackled both it was all the chips in the pot now, and the winner would be announced tonight she was having a campaign party.

After a not-so-smooth day of preliminary trials, she was almost ready to quit both. As she stepped out of the courtroom flanked by an assistant D.A. and a paralegal both with arms full of files, she stopped short when she found herself face to face with Stewart and Jones.

"You two go ahead, I'll meet you at the office." She said to her co-workers. She turned her attention to the detectives. "I assume you're here because you have a break in the case?"

Stewart removed a business card from the outer pocket of her suit jacket. She handed it to Veronica. "Not exactly."

Veronica looked at it skeptically. "It's my business card and?"

"And we got it from a con named Parker Harris."

Veronica sucked her teeth. "Are we going somewhere with this detective or are we going to prolong it with fragmented statements?"

"He says you're his lawyer."

Veronica didn't respond, she stared at the two blankly. Stewart continued. "Just checking all possible leads counselor."

"Mr. Harris is a person of interest, how so?"

"Didn't say him."

"Are you two going to get to it stop wasting my time."

"We went to see senator Tyner; he was attacked and I'm not sure if you're aware or not, but the senator is the father of Charles Tyner who is a person of interest been on the run for the past few years."

"Are you going somewhere with this?" Veronica turned from Stewart and faced Jones. "Is she going somewhere with this?"

Jones cleared his throat. "It's our theory that it is too big of a coincidence that Black Love gets back to town, the murders ramp up, and the senator is attacked and almost killed."

Veronica laughed. "You're saying that somehow Harris, Love, and Tyner conspired to kidnap, mutilate, and murder these girls? What proof do you have?"

"It's like I said, it's a working theory."

Veronica began walking again, the detectives followed keeping pace. "It's less of a theory and more like a fantasy novel, where are we with forensics? Questioning the lone survivor from the hospital? Deciphering the messages left carved into the victims, this perp is begging for you guys to catch him. Are you two working on any of these things? You know anything that looks like actual police work?"

Stewart placed her hand on Veronica's shoulder. "All due respect counselor we didn't come here for you to tell us how to do our jobs."

Floyd Sr.

Veronica looked down at the detective's hand, then back to her face sternly. Stewart removed her hand and placed them in her pockets. Veronica spoke. "Do your jobs detectives and bring me results, with the media, and social media shining a light in Chicago the world is watching." Veronica continued her way as the two detectives stood watching her walk away.

***

Chapter Forty-Eight

Erica laughed to herself as she walked down the halls of the hospital wearing the nurses' scrubs. The entire situation was like something straight out of a cheesy Lifetime movie. She purposely chose the uniform a size too small and wore a push-up bra to divert attention to her chest. Men were so easily distracted; she approached the senator's room with two cups of coffee in hand. She sipped from one and handed the other to the officer guarding the door.

"What's this?" He asked as he accepted the cup.

She smiled flirtingly. "Just starting my shift, stopped by Starbucks before coming in, they messed up my drink and made another said I could have both. I'm gifting to you, you're welcome."

He took a sip from the cup as she continued into senator Tyner's room. She stood in front of the door staring at the senator lying in bed in recovery from surgery. He lies in bed with bandages and tubes sticking out of his arms and mouth. Making her way to his bedside she placed her coffee cup on the stand near his bed, she leaned over and licked the side of his face.

"You lucky old bastard."

Tyner pleaded with his eyes just as she placed a pillow over his face and held it there until she felt no more fight in him. She removed the pillow to find his dead blue eyes staring back at her. She placed the pillow behind his head, closed his eyelids, and folded his hands on top of his chest as if he were asleep. She left the room, flirted with the officer for a few minutes then made her way to the elevator just as Stewart and Jones were stepping off the doors were closing, and Jones placed his hand into the elevator holding the doors open for her. She smiled at the detective after stepping on she winked, and the doors closed.

***

Chapter Forty-Nine

Black dialed Parker, it rang until voicemail picked up. Black left a message. "Let me know if you left for Clarksdale or not, I know we had that disagreement, but I need to know if you're still working the case with me…call me back bro."

He sat at a table in his area of the armory, an old school radio sat on the table station tuned to 107.5, he had it on just for background noise the radio personality was talking about the radio station making donations to the fraternal order of police encouraging the listeners to make donations as well, there was a campaign celebration taking place at the convention center, Erica Vice of the Planned Parenthood of Canada as well as others were making donations. His mind was jumping from situation to situation: Veronica would be at her celebration party, he was confident that she would win, and wonder if she asked Parker to go with her. He laughed. That would be an awkward situation, police are not his favorite people. Would things ever get right with him and Parker again? Where exactly did he stand with Stone? Where did he stand with Trigger? Would they ever find the killers and if they would find any of the girls alive? "Where have you two been all morning?" Black asked as Stewart and Jones entered the call center.

"Long morning Love, don't start," Jones said as he picked up a paper cup and pot of coffee pouring himself a cup.

"Look when I was asked to come on to this case, I didn't expect us all to be a loving family and such, but I thought we'd throw each other a bone here and there."

Stewart and Jones eyed one another, neither saying a word. Black looked to Stewart then back to Jones. "Is that a no, we won't be sharing information, or is it that you two don't have anything to share?"

"What do you got?" Jones asked flopping down in a chair across from Stewart who stood in front of him.

Black smirked. "Never mind, you don't want to share your toys I'm not sharing mine," Black said as he headed towards the exit.

"Wait a minute, where are you going?" Stewart demanded.

Black spoke with his back to the two detectives as he continued walking. "I'm starting from the beginning."

The two detectives shrugged and watched as Black exited the call center.

Jones stared at Stewart for a beat before speaking.

"What is wrong with you?" He asked as his partner stared off into the distance with a quizzical smile.

"What do you mean?"

"What's the obsession with Love and his partner?"

"You don't trust your instincts anymore?"

"I do when there is some foundation or rhyme or reason pointing me in that direction but this ain't that."

Stewart didn't respond, she opened a file on her desk and began thumbing through the pages until she found the one, she was looking for, she opened her phone and dialed a number.

"Who are you calling?"

"Give me a minute alright."

***

Chapter Fifty

Parker had made good time making his way back to Chicago, he managed to avoid all the heavy traffic coming into the city he knew he'd have to face the situation with Black sooner than later he picked up his phone and dialed his number after a few rings it was answered.

"What's good?" Black said through the phone on the other end.

"Shit, just getting back home went to see the old man in Clarksdale."

"How did that go?"

"Might be something, might not."

"Yeah?"

"Yeah, the old man is a retired mortician, who taught Jon everything he knows."

"Makes sense, that would explain how he knows his way around a body with a knife without having a medical degree."

"I was thinking the same thing, but that doesn't explain the other bodies being butchered."

"Back to my original theory, there have to be two killers."

"Man, you think any of this has to do with Charles, it all seems different in some way, know what I mean?"

"Yeah, but if not him, who? I mean why is my name in this know what I'm saying?"

"Yeah, what about his girl?"

"Avery? I mean, the tub had her blood DNA all over it and a body was never found police assumed she became another victim he chopped up and ate."

"I don't know man, where you at, where we at with the Franklins?"

"I'm headed over to the precinct to go over all the evidence from the beginning and the Franklins, haven't gotten back with them yet, having Bunchy check in with the other girl's families to see if any of those girls are missing."

"Cool, I'm sitting down the block from Jon's ex-wife's place going to knock on the door in a few, want to get a feel for the block first."

"Parker."

"Yeah."

"Are we good?"

"We're good."

There was a silent pause. Black spoke again. "Touch down with you in a few hours."

"Bet."

Parker ended the call.

***

Chapter Fifty-One

Everything was a bloody mess, literally and figuratively laying at his feet was his ex-wife's lover marinading in his blood, one hand loosely laying on top of Jon's foot, the bloody blade held firmly in Jon's fist. Standing in the dark, only the sound of his heartbeat and jumbled thoughts keeps him company.

"What did I do? She finds out I did this she will hate me forever."

Jon took a breath, took a step back, and looked down at the cause of all his pain, his face morphed into a scowl. He took another step back and paused. Footsteps above his head, he held his breath. Tip-toed to the foot of the stairs. Listened as he heard the footsteps become distant. Crept up the stairs, gently cupping the doorknob and twisting, nudging it open, he caught a glance of the back of his ex-wife's head as she rounded the corner.

The excitement of almost being caught emboldened him, he closed the door and followed in her path stepping lightly. Pausing at the bottom of the stairs leading to the second floor, he stood staring, he placed his right foot, on the bottom step. Paused. Took a step back and headed back out the way that he had entered humming Sam Cooke's "A Change is Gonna Come" as he strolled down the block and around the corner feeling triumphant that he had gotten away, down the street Parker turned on the engine to his car and began creeping towards him.

***

Chapter Fifty-Two

"What is this fool up to?" Parker says as his car creeps along the road, giving Salt time to make it to his vehicle so he can follow him. As his car rounds the corner his path is blocked by a squad car he brakes and hears the chirp of another squad car behind him. He looks in the rearview mirror, places the car in park, and turns off the engine, ignoring the cars approaching his vehicle he watches as Salt gets into his van and pulls off.

One of the officers approaches his window, and the other he sees through his rearview mirror is standing behind his car staring through the window with his hand on his gun. Parker shifts his attention to the officer approaching, he rolls down his window.

"Is there a problem officer?"

"We got a call that a suspicious man was sitting in his car, they said you didn't live around here."

"It's against the law to sit in a parked car?"

"You have licenses and insurance?"

Parker reached above his visor and removed his insurance card, removed his wallet from his pants, and handed him his licenses and insurance.

"You sit tight, I'll be right back."

The officer went back to his squad car, Parker watched the other officer through the rearview mirror their eyes locked. The two had a stare-down until the other officer returned and they both drew their weapons and had them aimed at Parker.

"Sir, get out of the car slowly with your hands up!"

Parker slowly opened the door and stepped out with his hands up. "Is all of this necessary?"

"Turn around and face the vehicle."

Parker did as he was instructed. "Man, y'all are tripping."

One of the officers holstered his weapon, approached Parker, and placed handcuffs on his hands behind his back.

"We have a warrant for your arrest."

"My arrests? I ain't did shit, arrests for what?"

"Parole violation. Assault on a peace officer, you got dinged in the system your P.O. issued the warrant you should never have been released, a mistake on our part we'll correct that right now partner call a tow company."

He led Parker to his squad car placed him in the backseat and closed the door.

***

Stewart pulled into the parking lot of the restaurant at 212 W. Fairchild in Danville, IL. It was a longshot, but it was the last thing she had in her arsenal on Black Love, she was there to meet Chief Waeltz he was the detective working the rape case of Black's ex back in the day she was there to pick his brain, maybe he might have some dirt on Black.

She got out of the car, slammed the door closed, and looked around, it was a nice crowd in the diner sitting at a table near the window she spotted the chief standing out proud and pristine in his white hat and uniform. She made her way to the table and offered her hand in a handshake.

"Thank you for taking the time to meet chief."

"No problem at all, it was just a ten-minute drive for me, you had to take the road trip and who am I to turn down a free meal and help a sister of the badge."

Stewart pulled her chair out and sat. A waitress appeared and placed a coffee mug on the table, she filled the cup and was off.

"You wanted to talk about District attorney Love?" Waeltz asked as he stirred sugar into his cup.

"Yes, he's no longer D.A."

"No."

"He stepped down shortly after leaving here."

"Interesting."

"How so?"

Waeltz tapped a finger on the table. The waitress returned with another cup and placed it on the table in front of Stewart, she filled her cup.

"Are you two ready to order or do you need a minute?" The waitress asked.

"Give us a minute Sara," Waeltz said as he took a sip from his cup. She nodded and was off. He continued. "Nothing really, he just didn't strike me as the quitting type."

"What type did he strike you as?"

"The dig-in, pain in my ass type."

They both laughed. "Chief, how was the backlash with the department after he and the Teresa Prince fiasco."

He shook his head and stared off into the distance. "It was never the same, it didn't help morale, left holes in the foundation I had to rebuild but eventually the department came through."

"With your leadership no doubt, you were a detective back then, right?"

"That's right, promoted, took over for Witherspoon there was no way they were going to continue to let him run things after the shit show that took place here. Why the big interests in a small-town history lesson? I'm sure you guys have plenty of shit going on in Chicago."

"Need anything you can give me on Love."

"Why is that?"

"My partner and I caught the New Trier girls' case."

"I read about that."

"Yeah, talking about pressure, my captain, the chief, and I can go on and on the higher up it goes the more the shit stinks."

"You have your eyes on Love for this?"

"There are implications that point in his direction."

"In other words, a fishing expedition."

"Not exactly sir I-"

"Don't bullshit me, detective."

"I wouldn't dream of it Chief."

Waeltz picked up the menu and looked at it. "Umm-hmm, during that shit show while he was down here there were a lot of things that didn't make the paper or the official reports."

"Such as?"

He set the menu down, and locked eyes with Stewart. "Any of this shit makes it to your official report or I hear from your Captain or Chief or some asshole D.A. I will not only deny it all and paint you as the liar you are I will-"

"I know, end my career."

"No, I would do something far worse."

Stewart sneered at Waeltz. He continued. "The things that didn't make it into the official report or any other place was that we had a mini shoot out here with some rogue cops and some of Love's people, our side lost."

"Why was it kept quiet?"

"I was met by some powerful people, don't know if Black was connected to them or not but they wanted it to go away, so it went away. A cop who Teresa pointed out as one of the officers who sexually assaulted her wound up dead in a separate incident that one, I would bet my pension was Love."

"It was never investigated?"

"What part of powerful people don't you understand?"

She threw her hands in the air. "Well, if I couldn't use any of this why tell me?" An alert came through her phone, she pulled it from her waist and looked at it. It was an email from forensics.

"You're a detective aren't you, figure it out." He raised his hand to flag down the waitress. "We're ready to order."

She stood from the table, removed cash from her pocket, and placed it on the table. "Enjoy your lunch chief thanks again for your time, I have a break in my case."

"Good luck detective." He said as she dashed out of the restaurant.

***

Chapter Fifty-Three

The convention center was shoulder to shoulder with police, politicians, local media, and celebrities Veronica moved around the room like floating on a cloud the winner had just been announced and champagne was flowing. Across the room she spotted a familiar face, she made her way over to her, and with a champagne flute in hand, they embraced with a hug and a kiss on the cheek.

"Ms. Vice, so nice to see you here."

"Please, call me Erica, are you ready to be the new Attorney General?"

"Yes ma'am!" Veronica said holding her glass in the air, as Erica held hers up as well and their glasses clanked. The two laughed as Veronica couldn't help but take notice once again of the scar going down Erica's arm.

"You know it's alright to ask."

"Ask what?" Veronica said turning her eyes away from Erica.

"The scar on my arm."

"Oh, I didn't mean to be rude and stare."

Erica ran her slender finger across the scar on her arm. "Yes, you did."

Veronica took a sip from her glass. Erica continued.

"Go ahead."

"Go ahead and what?"

"Ask me, what happened to my arm."

"It's none of my business."

"That does not mean that you do not want to know."

"Some other time perhaps."

"Perhaps."

Veronica gave a head nod and made her way across the room to the police captain in charge of the New Trier case.

"Captain."

"Madame General Attorney."

She smiled. "Enjoying the evening?"

"Only just got here."

"Well, more good news to go with the win, I just got a text from detectives Stewart and Jones that they may have a lead in the case."

"Yeah."

"The dead senator, the labs sent in the results from they're from Avery Gillian."

"The son's girlfriend, I thought she was presumed deceased?"

"There was not a body that was ever recovered, and she was a suspect in the missing girls' cases from the south side, she worked at the abortion clinic where all the girls were connected. There's been an APB placed on her."

"Think she'll lead us to him or the New Trier girls?"

"That's what we're hoping."

***

Chapter Fifty-Four

Sprawled across the floor of his office Black had copies of crime scene photos from the beginning of the case until now, on the other side of the room sprawled across the floor were crime scene pictures of the body parts found in the freezer and the bathtub where Avery's blood was found he was looking to see if there was a connection between the two.

He knelt, and picked up one of the photos of the torso of a teenage girl, just the midsection. No head. No arms. No legs. Just her breasts and stomach. Carved into her stomach with a knife were the words- Unfinished Business- Black Love XOXO

He stared at the photo for several seconds imagining what type of blade could have been used to cut into the girl. He set the photo down and picked up another. Lying on a table the right arm of one girl and the left arm of another. They were visibly different even in the photo you could tell that they didn't belong to the same person one was three inches longer than the other. Scribbled underneath each arm were the names of each victim that the arms belonged to, stapled to the back of the photo were copies of fingerprints taken from the National Child Identification Program, a network that parents voluntarily have their children fingerprinted, and those prints are stored into a database and used in child abduction cases. These were the only two children whose parents had their fingerprints stored in the database.

Black set the photos back onto the floor stood and went over to his desk picked up a manilla folder and opened it, Dexter and

Jennifer Hall parents of the right-arm girl. He dropped the folder back to his desk, picked up the other, and opened it to James and Julie Benz parents of the left-arm girl. Neither parent had any connection to the other parents other than their children went to the same school and were on the cheerleader team together.

He had gone over their arrest records, well one arrest record only Julie had been arrested before, petty theft back in college. Other than that, the Halls and Benz's were clean. He had copies of their bank statements they were all earning seven digits or higher no debt.

He placed the folder back on his desk turned back to the crime scene photos and let his eyes scan the floor looking at the photos trying to see if anything stood out. He stood over another photo on the floor, crouched down, and read the inscription carved into the girl's stomach: Ning Cai, Söze & Ehrich Weiss- Black Love XOXO. He stood. Heard the door downstairs open and close, he ignored it thinking it was Parker coming in.

He heard footsteps coming up the steps with his back to the door he kept scanning the papers on the floor.

"What's up, Black?"

He turned at the sound of the familiar voice. "What are you doing here Trigger?"

"I thought I'd surprise you and Parker and take you out to lunch, I still have the key from when I was working here it's not a problem is it?"

Black shook his head no. "Keep it for emergencies, going to have to pass on going out for lunch have to figure this out. Besides Parker is out running down a lead."

She stared down at the files scattered all over the floor and desk. "What is all of this?"

"Evidence from the New Trier case and evidence from the missing girls' case a few years back."

She squatted and picked up the photo with Ning Cai, Söze & Ehrich Weiss- Black Love XOXO etched into the torso. "I saw this on the internet."

"Sick bastard."

"Erick Vice"

"What? Erick Vice, that's how you pronounce it, it's German."

"You took German?"

"Yeah, I didn't tell you that?"

"You know damn well you didn't tell me that."

She laughed. "Hmm."

His forehead wrinkled. "Erick Vice huh?" He went to his desk, pushed papers to the side, and opened his laptop. Keyed in Ehrich Weiss. "It says here that it was the birth name of Harry Houdini."

She walked around the desk and stood behind Black leaning over his shoulder and reading the screen. "A magician and a murder sound like the title of a cheesy mystery novel."

"Whoever this is their taunting me, they want me to catch them!"

She rubbed his shoulders and let her hands run down his chest. "Don't overthink it."

He opened another window on his computer and keyed in Ning Cai. It popped up on the screen, and they both read in silence.

"Another magician?" Trigger said moving Black's hand from the mouse and scrolling down to read the rest of the article.

"Yeah, but she's from Singapore."

"How are these two connected other than magic tricks?"

"Scroll back up." Trigger did as he said. He read aloud. "It says that she's an illusionist and she also wrote a book."

Trigger stepped away from the computer and began pacing the room. "What's the name of her book?"

"It's called Misdirection."

Trigger and Black both laughed. "A bit on the nose, right?"

"I was thinking the same thing," Black said as he stood from the desk.

"You aren't going to look up the last name?"

He shook his head no. "Nah, I know it."

"You do? Someone, you know?"

"Not personally...the greatest trick the devil ever pulled was convincing the world he was dead."

"Bible scriptures?"

Black laughed. "Nope. Usual Suspects Kevin Spacey said those words when he played Keyser Söze."

"Never seen it."

"You never seen Usual Suspects?"

"Nope."

"You're kidding, right? Kevin Spacey, Benicio Del Toro, Stephen Baldwin, Giancarlo Esposito."

Trigger shrugged.

"We have to have a movie night when this is all over, great movie."

"If you say so, focus Black what's the connection?"

"I am focused, we have two magicians and a fictional character all signed to me."

"What about nationalities?"

"If there's a connection, I don't see it we have an Asian, a German, and a line from an American actor."

Trigger continues pacing they both remain silent eyes scanning evidence. Trigger flops down in the chair. Black picks up the photo with Ning Cai, Söze & Ehrich Weiss- Black Love XOXO.

"How do you pronounce the German name again?"

"Erick Vice."

Black began laughing.

"What?"

"That cocky, arrogant bitch."

"Who?"

"I know who the killer is."

She stood, as he walked out of the room and ran down the stairs. She ran behind. "Wait for me." They continued out of the house and got into his car. "You want to fill me in on what's going on?"

Black started the car and pulled off. He dialed Parker; it went straight to voicemail. "Parker, I know who the killer is, where are you at? Call me back bruh." He ended the call. "The first name on the list is Ning Cai, right?"

"Yeah, it says she is a magician."

"Well, it says she is an illusionist. That was our first clue, an illusion is a deceptive appearance or impression…a false idea or belief right makes you think you see something that's not there."

"Right."

"The second clue was a part of the first clue; it says that she wrote a book, right?"

"Yeah, it was called Misdirection."

Black laughed again. "That one was another taunt from the old case, the two are connected. I'll explain that one later."

"And the rest of the clues?"

"Söze, the quote was: the greatest trick the devil ever pulled was convincing the world he was dead, another quote to rub my nose in it."

"I am lost, Black."

"Just bear with me, I'm getting to it. The last was Ehrich Weiss."

"Yes."

"I've heard that name before."

"From where?"

"A colleague Veronica Malone."

"Parker's girl?"

"Yeah, you two met?"

"Something like that."

Black continued driving, looking at Trigger from the corner of his eye waiting for her to elaborate when he saw that she wasn't he continued. "She kept telling me that a big contributor to her campaign wanted to meet me her name was Erica Vice."

"That's too big of a coincidence Vice is not a common last name."

"I know."

"Where are we going?"

"Veronica's celebration party."

***

Chapter Fifty-Five

Standing at the entrance to the hall where the celebration was being held, Black thought he was going to have a harder time getting in but when he flashed his old badge from when he was DA and the officer at the door barely gave it a second look, he and Trigger marched right in.

"Are you sure she'll be here?" Trigger asked, her eyes scanning the room.

"She's here."

"What does she look like?"

"I'll know her when I see her."

"That doesn't help me, Black."

"You take that part of the room, look for Veronica, and tell her what's going on she knows what she looks like."

"How do you know she hasn't already left?"

"Just find Veronica," Black said as he began walking towards the other side of the room eyes darting from face to face. He weaved in between people wearing tuxedos, thousand-dollar suits, and women in short skirts, high heels, and gowns. He looked across the room once more and locked eyes with Trigger, Veronica was on the side of her whispering to the chief, seconds later he was moving from officer to officer whispering in their ears Black watched the scene play out as the officers in the room began moving towards the exits in what Black assumed was them being covert, they were about to initiate a lockdown but wanted the exits secured before they announced it.

What Black didn't know is that Erica was standing behind him, she smirked and passed to the left of him through the crowd and out of the room before the exit she was near was secured. Black met with Veronica and Trigger across the room.

"How sure are you about this Love?" the chief asked.

"It's her," Black said confidently. His phone vibrated in his pocket. He pulled it out and looked at it. "Let's go." He demanded without looking back. The trio followed behind as they all marched from the hall until they were outside, standing in front of them was Erica Vice in handcuffs, with Bunchy standing behind her.

"She did exactly what you said she would do Black, she walked right into my hands."

Black stepped up to Erica so that he was face to face. He laughed. "Finally got you."

"You've gotten something, I'm not sure we know what that is yet, but I suspect we'll find out soon enough."

"Get her down to the station." The chief says as he climbs into the passenger seat of Bunchy's car.

"Can you get me in on that interrogation?" Black asks facing Veronica.

"Of course."

"Have you heard from Parker?"

"Not since last night."

"You two alright?"

She began walking in the opposite direction. "Meet you at the station."

"You going with me?" Black asked Trigger now that the two were alone.

"Enough excitement for me for the night." She kissed Black. "I'll get an Uber home, call me once you get settled."

"Be careful," Black says as he dashes toward where he parked his car.

***

Chapter Fifty-Six

"Call me back bruh, you said next time I make a move keep you in the loop, I'm reaching out hit me back damn." Black ended the call and paused at the interrogation door. Veronica, Jones, Stewart, and Bunchy were all standing there.

"What's going on?" Black asked, wondering why no one was in there questioning her.

"She says she will only speak to you and me," Veronica says looking confused.

"Let me go in then," Black says stepping forward, Jones placed his hand on Black's chest. Black grabbed his wrist and twists it bending it backward, Jones twists his body to get out of the uncomfortable situation and drops to his knees.

"No more free passes Jones since day one I've been telling you to keep your hands off of me."

Stewart places her hand on her gun but doesn't pull it, she locks eyes with Black. The rest of the officers in the room are frozen in place waiting to see what their next move should be. Veronica places her hand on Black's shoulder.

"Let him go, we don't have time for this right now."

Black releases his wrists and steps around him and pushes the door open into the interrogation room. Veronica follows behind and closes the door behind her. One arm is handcuffed to the table; Veronica begins a slow clap.

"Congratulations Black, you figured it out."

"Where are the girls?" Black said as he stepped forward and placed his hands on the table.

"Just rush right in and stick it in huh? Can't a girl get a little foreplay first?"

"I'm not playing games with you."

"I'm not playing with you either private dick."

There was a knock at the door, then it was opened, Tyler Takashi-Diaz stepped in and closed the door behind him.

"Are you alright?" He asked as he pulled a chair and sat next to Erica.

"I'm fine."

"Tyler, what are you doing here?"

"I texted him to meet me here when I saw Black and his Lil girlfriend come in I knew you were on to me," Erica said as she placed her hand on top of Tyler's.

"What are you saying, are you admitting to the New Trier girls?" Veronica asked pulling a chair out and sitting across from the two.

Tyler held up his hand. "Whoa, she isn't admitting anything...yet."

"Are you, her attorney?" Black asked standing behind Veronica.

"No," Tyler said as he removed his phone and sent a text, and seconds later the door opened, and her attorney walked in. "This is her attorney."

A barely five-foot-tall, petite, blonde-haired woman walked in wearing gray pants suit carrying a briefcase. She closed the door behind her and set the briefcase on the table.

"I'm Kelly Rose, I have been retained as legal counsel for Ms. Dumas."

"Who the hell is Dumas? It isn't Erica Vice? Or Avery Gillian? I'm starting to lose track here." Black asked as he remained standing, now leaning against the wall.

"You will refer to my client by her birth name Genevieve Dumas, she is a Canadian-French citizen with an American work visa. Ms. Dumas legally changed her name to Avery Gillian when she came to America years ago, she has since changed it back to Genevieve Dumas. I have all the proper paperwork here." Kelly pulled papers from her briefcase and placed them in front of Veronica.

"Fine, Ms. Dumas we will be recording during the duration of this interrogation."

"Before you turn on the recorder may we have a word," Tyler said as he stood and stepped over to a corner on the other side of the room. Veronica stood and joined him. He leaned close so that he spoke into her ear. "That favor that I said I would be coming for…this is it."

She whispered in his ear. "I told you I wouldn't cover for your illegal shit."

"Technically you said no organized crime and you agreed are you not a woman of your word?"

Her nose flared, and she rolled her eyes and returned to her seat.

"Fine. Before I turn this tape recorder on, I need it all, how it was done, why, and the locations of any other missing girls that we don't know about starting with the location of the missing girls now!"

Erica looked to her lawyer, her lawyer looked to Veronica, and Veronica rolled her eyes and continued. "In exchange for that Genevieve Dumas will get full immunity from prosecution of any all present or previous crimes including murder."

"What? You have to be kidding Veronica!" Black said as he slid his chair back.

"I've got this Black." She turned her attention back to Erica. "Do we have an agreement?"

Erica nodded. "Pen and paper please."

Veronica slid the items over to Erica; she began jotting down information on the paper. Veronica pressed the record on the recorder.

Veronica continued. "This is the address to a warehouse that I own in Gary, IN it's where the remaining girls are."

Veronica looked up at the two-way mirror, a few seconds later the door opened, and she handed the slip of paper over to Jones.

"That's all my client has to say until something is formally drawn up." Kelly Rose said as she scrolled through her cell phone and placed it into her briefcase.

"Fine." Veronica stood, removed her phone, and made a phone call. She glared at Tyler and then exited the room.

***

Chapter Fifty-Seven

Black and Veronica waited outside the interrogation room talking, Veronica had paralegals drawing up the terms of the immunity agreement she was waiting for them to arrive with the documents. Tyler stood across the room waiting as well, he stepped out of the interrogation room to give Erica and her attorney privacy to talk.

"Tell me again why you did this?"

"It's not going to change Black; the answer is still going to be the same, he helped me get into office, I knew he was going to want his pound of flesh, didn't know what it would be but figured whatever it was I could handle it. I sure as hell didn't expect him to come to collect this soon or a price this severe."

"I know what is done is done, damn is it worth it?"

"If we can get these girls home without any more casualties and I still have my seat it'll have to be worth it. We'll get Erica Vice…Avery Gillian or whatever else she wants to go by another time, and you can bet your sweet ass we'll get her again."

The elevator doors opened, and a young blonde-haired girl stepped off carrying a manila folder, she spotted Veronica and rushed towards her arm stretched out. Veronica met her halfway and retrieved the file from her. "Thank you, everything good in here? No time for me to check your work." Veronica said as she turned and began heading towards the interrogation room.

"Yes ma'am, had another paralegal double check on the ride over its ironclad."

Veronica pushed the door open and walked in, she was followed by Black and Tyler. She dropped the file on the table and Kelly opened it and began reading. Ten minutes later it was signed, the recorder was on, and Erica was giving the details.

"You know I tried to forget this place, forget what I was taken through. But no matter how hard I tried the city was beckoning me to return. I couldn't bring myself to do it as before, it was boring." She flipped her hair and rolled her eyes. Continued. "Being at the abortion clinic made it easy with the endless supply of young black girls that the city ignored and mistreated." She laughed. "But the young white privileged girls, the same girls that ridiculed me growing up, they were even easier."

There was a tap at the door and was opened, Veronica and Black both turned to see who had opened the door. It was Bunchy standing next to Jon's ex; her face was puffy and swollen from crying. Black recognized her from her social media files, she looked a little older, but it was her. He stood. "Give me a sec."

He stepped out of the room closing the door behind him. Bunchy pulled him to the side.

"She found her boyfriend dead in her basement she didn't see who did it but she's convinced it was her ex, said he's been calling and harassing them."

"Jon Salt."

"Yeah, Jones and Stewart just radioed in and said they found the warehouse and some of the girls still alive, Salt was there he was in on it with Vice, they're headed back now. I'm going to put her in an interrogation room and see if she needs anything to eat."

"Thanks for keeping me in the loop man."

Bunchy nodded. Black went back into the room and sat.

"What I want to know is, why the need to taunt me?" Black asked as soon as he entered the room.

"Everything was perfect before you came along, Charles, my sweet Charles."

"Where is Charles, was he in on this with you?" Veronica asked interrupting her confession.

"Charles, no not at all." She ran her finger along the scar on her arm.

Black leaned back in his seat. "Charles is gone, isn't he?"

Erica smiled. Then her face morphed into a picture of sadness.

"Yes, Black he's gone never to be seen again."

"The tub was covered with your DNA...your blood, it was in the tub, invisible to the naked eye but revealed with a black light it was everywhere. We ran a sample from the tub against a sample of yours on file with the state. It was a match, assumed you were dead, that Charles had you know..."

"Eaten me?" Erica said once again running her finger along her scar.

"How did she do it?" Veronica asked looking for clarification.

Black reached out and grabbed her arm. "The answer is right here. I guess that Charles was never there. She cut into her arm and doused the tub with blood, cleaned it, and left. Charles was either already dead and then she ate him, or she killed him and got rid of the body, either way, she knew with him missing and her DNA in the tub it would look like he had killed her and fled the city. Söze- the greatest trick the devil ever pulled was convincing the world he was dead."

"Where is he?" Veronica asked.

"He's dead, unfortunately, there is no way that I can prove it you'll just have to take my word for it."

"What about the girls from the south side?"

"Yes, Charles and I had taken the girls and had our way with them, to put it mildly."

"What about the missing mixed girl- half black half Asian her name was Layus."

"Doesn't ring a bell," Genevieve said looking confused.

"We need a list of all of the girls." Veronica placed a pad and pen in front of Erica. They stood to leave. They opened the door, and Veronica paused and turned back. "Don't leave anything off, we find out about anything after the fact the immunity deal is dead and you will be arrested, tried, and convicted."

Just before she spoke, she looked up and saw a group of girls dressed in dirty torn, and ragged cheerleader uniforms walk past. Behind the group of girls was Jon, in handcuffs. Jones who was leading him stopped in front of the door.

"There was one more girl, Kia Salt, I believe was her name." Erica licked her lips. "Now that girl was scrumptious, I savored every bite." She locked eyes with Salt and laughed. "Every time I would come across something about her online asking for tips about where she was, I would think about how much I enjoyed her, and my mouth would water all over again."

Salt yanked away from the detective and charged towards the room, he didn't make it far before he was hit with a stun gun and fell to the floor. A group of officers picked him up and carried him away. Veronica placed her hand on her temples. She looked at Tyler. "My debt with you is cleared, the next time I cross paths with you Erica Vice there will be handcuffs on you."

"I doubt it will play out that way, but I look forward to us chatting again madam Attorney General."

"Shaunte Franklin, and the others…why?"

"Let's call it OCD- I hate leaving things undone."

Black glared at Genevieve then he and Veronica step into the hall.

"This doesn't sit right with me."

"We got the girls back, got one of the killers, and we'll get the mastermind soon enough."

Black laughed. "Mastermind huh? If she's the villain, what does that make us?"

"Today, it makes us the victors."

"If you say so, it feels like a loss to me."

"She does not get to win, we are the United States Government, one way or another we always have the last say."

"You hear from Parker tell him to reach out to me," Black said as he stepped on the elevator and a young man clean-shaven, not a hair out of place wearing an expensive suit stepped off and approached Veronica.

"Madame Attorney General, congratulations on your win. I am Perry Pearce, I'm then-new prosecutor, I can take over from here with the Dumas case."

Veronica's phone rang, and she stepped away. Then came back to Perry after finishing her call. "I know you have a lot of things on your plate, but I was wondering if I could ask something of you."

"What is that?"

"That was an associate of mine, to be honest, more than an associate. His name is Parker Harris, he's been arrested on a parole violation."

"What was the charge?"

"Assault on an officer."

"And what would you like for me to do?"

"He's a good guy, caught a bad break caught in a situation he didn't ask for, he may get sent back behind this one."

"Are you ordering me to intervene?"

"You know I can't do that; I wouldn't do that if I could."

"What are you asking me?"

"Do me a favor and give this guy a second chance."

"I don't know the particulars of his case but if he's out on parole the state of Illinois has already given him a second chance and he abused it. If I'm being honest ma'am if you ask me to do this I will, I won't like it, but I will if you insist if I am to do my job and do what's best for the citizens of Illinois I'm going to pass. Which is it, Attorney General Malone?"

She sighed. "Thank you for your time, I'll see you around."

She walked off before he could respond.

***

Chapter Fifty-Eight

Black sat back on his sofa Sade's greatest hits playing in the background, incense burning, reading Thomas Sowell's "Discrimination and Disparities". This was the first time he had alone time in a long time. It had been two days since the New Trier girls had been returned, and he had to give the bad news to the Franklins and the other parents of the black girls that went missing. He knew it wasn't his job to do so but felt it would be better coming from him than the police. After never hearing from Parker or Veronica he finally reached out to people he knew who worked at the county and found out that Parker had been violated back, he was waiting to be transferred back to Joliet prison to complete the remainder of his sentence. His phone vibrated on the table next to him he picked it up, a number he didn't recognize, and he pressed the talk button.

"Black." The voice on the other end of the phone said.

"Speaking, who is this?"

"Crishan, you said I can reach out if I need you?"

"Yeah."

"I'm reaching out."

"What do you need?"

"Can't speak about it on the phone, but wear old clothes, and bring gloves I'm texting you the address."

The call ended. A few seconds later a text came through. Black looked at the address, threw on old black sweatpants and sweat jacket, and old workout shoes, and grabbed a pair of old work gloves. He was out the door and forty minutes later pulling into a parking lot of an old mechanic's garage. He spotted Crishan pushing the sliding doors open. Black crept into the garage and turned his car off. He watched Crishan through his rearview mirror as he closed the door. He climbed out of the car putting his gloves on.

"What's up man, you all covert and shit, what you need me to get rid of a body or something?" Black laughed.

Crishan didn't. He continued walking without speaking, across the garage with Black following until he reached another door. Crishan pushed the door open and stepped to the side. Black stepped inside the room, to find Genevieve tied to a chair and bludgeoned to death.

"She said she didn't know what happened to my sister, I didn't like her answer especially since there was video surveillance of her sick fuck of a boyfriend leaving with her. So, to answer your question, yes, I do need help getting rid of a body are you carrying the arms or legs?"

The End

***

Sneak Peek
The Detective and the Criminal
A Black Love Detective Story Book 5

Chapter One

In an abandoned house in a West Englewood neighborhood at 5. am. three gunshots rang out from a Glock- two to the heart, one to the head execution-style he slumped over. His executioner grabbed a garbage bag filled with bundles of hundred-dollar bills. She dropped the gun on top of the cash. Stepped around the man and grabbed a leather bag filled with disposable cell phones.

"I thought you were laying low?" Vernon said as he scrolled through his phone.

"I am there was no way he wasn't going to the police or Lil G Man people, he had to go I'll reach out in a few days with a new number stay out of trouble until then."

"I'm a grown man fifty plus years old I don't need you telling me to stay out of trouble."

She laughed. "If you say so, Vernon."

"How many years it's been since you been gone?"

"Too many to mention, but not long enough for folks with a chip on their shoulder the size of the Sears Tower to forget."

"The Willis Tower."

"What?"

"It ain't been the Sears Tower for years."

"Fuck all that, it's always the Sears Tower in my eyes."

"Where are you going?"

"To see my son, outsource some work to him."

***

Chapter Two

For better or worse he was here now, started with a partner now he was riding solo, for a little while anyway until Parker came home. It had been three months since he had been violated back to Joliet to serve the remainder of his time, he had spent most of that time in Cook County, and the fact that he made it back to Joliet as soon as he had was a miracle most spent a year or more waiting to be transferred to their new home. Black had yet to take on another case but promised himself whatever he earned he would still split the profit with Parker.

He went to the office every day waiting for a call, now and then someone stopped in but either the case didn't interest him, they couldn't afford the rates, or they were just curious about the business being on the block. People in the neighborhood were getting used to seeing him there. They often asked for Parker, at one point he was there a lot more than Black was. He had a deal with the lady across the street, Ms. Jones he would join her for a game of Tonk once a week and she would keep an eye out for his business and call him if anything suspicious happened. He figured it was her way of feeling useful and she could probably use the company so after a bit of arguing that it wasn't necessary, he conceded.

He sat in the waiting area reading *"Nigger: The Strange Career of a Troublesome Word"* by Randall Kennedy. The doorbell rang, and Black stood and made his way to the door he opened the door to find a teenage boy about the same height as him, with red hair, freckles, scruffy beard. He had the bluest eyes staring back at Black.

"Can I help you?" Black asked staring at the young boy, it was strange to see a white kid in this neighborhood.

"Looking for work."

Black laughed. "Yeah, what kind of work do you do?"

"Whatever might need to be done."

Black looked around the boy to see if he was alone or not. "What are you doing around here? Where are your people at?"

"I'll do whatever you need, just trying to do the right thing and make a few bucks."

Black reached into his pocket and pulled out five twenty-dollar bills. He handed them to the boy. "Here."

The boy took it and looked at it strangely. "What's this for?"

"Nothing, I don't have anything for you to do around here, but you can have the money."

The boy attempts to give the money back. "I have to earn it; my uncle Mickey says ain't nothing in life free- sooner or later someone will come to collect a debt and I may not like the interests."

Black laughed. "Your uncle Mickey sounds like a smart man."

"He has his moments. So, what work do you have for me?"

"Look kid, my word as a man you don't owe me anything."

The kid stuffed the money into his pocket, nodded at Black then turned to leave. Black closed the door and went back to reading his book. Ten minutes later the bell was rung again, and the door opened. He thought it may have been Trigger, his on-again-off-again "friends" with benefits, or Pops, his father. He stood to go and meet the unannounced guest. He froze in his tracks when he spotted the person.

"Pepper Red."

She smiled. "That's how you address your mama now?"

Black stared mouth open.

"You hate me so much I can't get a hug?"

Black slowly walked toward his mother and wrapped his arms around her. Hugged her as tight as he could. "What are you doing here ma?"

"Long story, but I missed you."

Black stepped back and took in everything that was his mother. She hadn't changed much. She was taller than he at average height for a man but tall for a woman. She was carrying more weight than he remembered but she was in her mid-fifties she still looked good. Light skinned damn near red skin complexion hence the nickname Pepper Red. Her hair was in crochet braids and looked like fire red yarn. She stepped in walking around the place taking it all in.

"Like the sign out front."

"Thanks."

"I see you got help too."

"You heard about Parker?"

"That boy you used to run around with, it was three of you, no not him. I'm talking about the little white boy pulling the lawnmower out from around back."

Black made his way outside to find the boy pouring gasoline into the lawnmower.

"What are you doing?"

"Earning my keep, I see the grass ain't been done in a while, I'll do the front and back and we'll call it even. I'll make sure I clean the grass up and put the mower back where I found it."

Black wanted to scold the boy for breaking into his garage but needed to see what his mother wanted. He nodded at the boy and went back inside, closing the door behind him.

"You been to see Pops?"

"Yeah, I saw the old man, he still ain't got rid of that old house."

"What are you doing back here Pepper Red?"

"Need to settle some old debts."

"It's been over twenty years ma."

"When the debt collector comes, you have to pay no matter how long it's been."

"I'm guessing you came to say hi, handle your business then bounce back out of town?"

"Something like that came to hire you."

Black laughed. "Stop playing ma."

She reached into a backpack she was carrying and removed two bundles of rolled-up hundred-dollar bills wrapped in rubber bands. She extended the money to him. He grabbed her by her wrist and examined the tattoo. He recognized the symbol; it was a figure eight on its side. The infinity symbol signified the concept of eternity.

"What's this?"

She yanked her arm away, ignoring his question. "Need you to find a man."

"What man, for what?"

"Either to clear my name or to kill him either way this ends before I leave Chicago."

***

About the Author

Antwan Floyd Sr. is an American novelist, most widely recognized for his crime fiction. He has written a series of best-selling mysteries featuring the hard-boiled detective Black Love, a black private investigator living in Chicago, IL; they are perhaps his most popular works.